About the author

Devanshi Sharma is twenty-two years and three books old. She loves talking about writing and has been invited as a speaker to many institutions, including SRCC and IIT Delhi, to judge their competitions. A dreamer by choice and a stubborn workaholic, for her, her family is her lifeline.

Hailing from the city of food, Indore, Devanshi is a total foodie and enjoys travelling while she is writing. Her previous book *No Matter What I Do* is a hot-selling read and continues to charm youngsters and elderly alike.

You can know more about her or get in touch with her at:

/authordevanshi @devanshiauthor devanshisharma.com

Praise for the author and her works

'She's making the write choice.'

– DNA

'A tantalising read...with soul-touching narrative.'

– The Times of India

'Unimaginably Talented.'

– Hindustan Times

'Dreams as a ray of hope: Devanshi.'

– The Chronicle, Raipur

Imperfect Misfits

DEVANSHI SHARMA

Srishti
PUBLISHERS & DISTRIBUTORS

Srishti Publishers & Distributors
Registered Office: N-16, C.R. Park
New Delhi – 110 019

Corporate Office: 212A, Peacock Lane
Shahpur Jat, New Delhi – 110 049
editorial@srishtipublishers.com

First published by
Srishti Publishers & Distributors in 2018

10 9 8 7 6 5 4 3 2

This is a work of fiction. The characters, places, organisations and events described in this book are either a work of the author's imagination or have been used fictitiously. Any resemblance to people, living or dead, places, events or organisations is purely coincidental.

Printed and bound in India

With the blessings of Radha Krishna, without whom, this book wouldn't have been possible!

Acknowledgments

Before even beginning with the acknowledgement, thank you for showering your love on *No Matter What I Do* and making it a bestseller. You've made my dream come true! Truly, readers make writers!

Then, coming to our *Imperfect Misfits*, the title very well defines the journey of the book as well. Out of the previous three books that I have written, this has been the most adventurous journey. And trust me, with all the waves of ups and downs, writing the acknowledgment is the most satisfying thing. Throughout this journey, those who stayed by my side ... a big thanks to them!

This book consists of some two hundred pages. Each page has a new story to narrate and each story is possible only because of the numerous efforts the most special people in my life have put in. First and foremost, my parents, without whom, forget this book, nothing in my life would have been possible. It is their zeal that keeps the restless soul in me motivated.

My grandparents and my family – I know handling a workaholic at home can be irritating and troublesome, but these guys love me the way I am.

My three younger best friends and the closest friends I have in life.

I'd actually like to thank each and every person with whom I have had a conversation about our book. Each day, talking of it makes me happier and inspires me to write more. So, to every person who has liked a Facebook post or messaged me, a big thank you!

The best people at workplace and the friends back in Indore, thank you! Without you hearing my endless blabber, this wouldn't have materialised the way this book has!

Last but not the least, I know I've troubled the team at Srishti a lot, so a big thanks to the brilliant team at Srishti! I am sure we'll cherish this time and all the experiences later.

Lastly, if I'd say I wrote the book in a moving Metro, it wouldn't be wrong. So, thanks to every single person who offered me a seat so I could write.

I'd just say what my favourite editor says, 'Thanks a ton'. :)

Prologue

How many times do we take a backseat from the day to day rush of our lives to stop and have a date with ourselves? We ask everyone how they are, but how many times have we asked ourselves the same thing? We keep tapping our phones to play and pause the playlist of songs as we travel, but how many instances do you remember of putting the whole world on hold to play the playlist of aims that you wish to achieve?

In rushing to office and in the zest of reaching on time, in rushing back from office in the zeal to get back home, in running to catch the earliest Metro or running to call out to a cab, perhaps the little wish inside the heart gets lost.

Before even reading Tiasha's story, take a minute, close your eyes and ask yourself,

'What do I want?'

First ten seconds, everything around you will seem to distract you, the next ten seconds your mind will suggest the materialistic pursuits of life (which by the way are important), however can be ignored for the time being. Finally, in the last few seconds of the second minute, that is, if you reach that point, you'll know what you really want.

Whatever you find in the final ten seconds – that is your answer. Could be as fun as being a joker or perhaps as serious as being a pilot, but whatever it is, it is your secret dream.

Take a minute, take an hour, or take a lifetime, but finding answer to this question is, well, exceptionally significant.

And, just before you judge this to be a self help book...

Part - I

Just like those freshly fried aloo tikkis

Travelling in a crowded Metro, bargaining with the shopkeepers at Sarojini Nagar, the huge statue of Lord Hanuman and the capture of the running Metro that features in all Indian television soaps, the sexy girls, the *tharki* boys, the Haryanvi accent, the rich Punjabi food – thanks to all the cinematographers of the Indian television, that's all we know of Delhi.

Bhaiya dilli toh dilwalon ka shehar hai. That's what we have heard repeatedly, *haina*?

Little did we know about a story brewing in the posh yet forgotten streets of West Delhi.

"Go straight for three hundred metres and turn right."

So ordered the lady we all speak to, almost every day, but whom we have never met – the Google girl. As she said so, Aakaash sat back in the comfortable Wagon R and fiddled with his phone. He had just entered the city of food, people, fights, and ... pollution, which was, by the way, his nest.

Taking the camera to the back seat of the Wagon R which was being driven by an old driver, let's zoom at the face sitting at the back seat. Dressed in a translucent yellow t-shirt and a pair of casual jeans; the square-framed, matte-finished spectacles which covered his extremely tranquil eyes; and a Samsung smartphone in his hand, Aakaash kept scrolling down, his eyes carefully reading the comments posted on a YouTube video.

He was so engaged in reading the comments that as soon as his phone rang, it almost slipped through his fingers. 'Startled' was the word to describe his expression at that moment.

Doesn't that happen at times? You are in a world where only you and your mobile phone exist. The moment someone tries to intervene, you're startled as if a glass of chilled water has been thrown on your face.

Similar was his case. In fact, every time he was in his zone, he just wanted to remain there.

He swiped his fingers over the smartphone screen to pick the call up.

"Where are you?" The voice from the other end asked authoritatively.

Soft yet firm, sugar-coated yet pampered – the voice perhaps was too familiar to him. Plus, the amount of authority this voice possessed evidently depicted that the person speaking from the other end held the right to be authoritatively his.

Resuming to his 'other' self and coming out of the world of videos, Aakaash replied, "Just waiting at the red light."

"Awesome. Get down at the juice corner and we'll go home together," she said cheerfully.

Husky, slightly shrill, but her voice was still soothing to his ears. The expression of happiness that he had on his face after listening to her explained it all.

While writing, I wonder how sometimes expressions speak more than words; the aroma of Biryani soothes and appetites the senses, and just some sound cures illness. Some things are beyond our understanding, aren't they?

As he ended the call, he wore a broad smile.

He knew very well why she wanted to welcome him so chirpily. He knew her voice was cheerful and the reason behind that cheerfulness was his arrival.

He also knew that she being there just when he was about to reach was no dramatic coincidence. She was there for him, to be with him. He knew her too well.

ᔓ

He got down and paid the cab driver, and saw her running towards him. Holding a chocolate with the wrapper torn off in her hands, she ran and directly landed the chocolate in his mouth.

Wrapping her arms around his neck, almost jumping on to him like a kid does to his mother, in a crowded market, she looked really excited. Aakaash smiled as he took a bite from the chocolate and said while wiping off the rest of it from his face, "You crazy monkey! Couldn't you wait till I'd taken my bag out?"

"Of course not," she said cutely with a bright smile.

Take the camera ten metres towards Aakaash's right, and there stood his best friend Tiasha. A pair of red cotton shorts, a loose crop top and hair tied in a tight bun made her look sporty. Add to that her by wide-black eyes with a brush of kohl and some gloss on her lips hiding their grayish colour – she was the girl next door, even literally, who was so special. She smiled broadly as she glanced continuously at his face.

What was the occasion for her to behave thus, you perhaps wonder?

Aakaash had posted his first video on YouTube after his first stand-up comedy gig in a college in Mumbai. The event might have been a few thousand kilometres away from Delhi, but Tiasha's senses were all concentrated on him throughout his trip.

She knew Aakaash wanted to be a stand up comedian, she knew being indifferently different was his dream and when she saw him take the first step towards his dream, she felt elated. The happiness on her face was genuine, almost as if his act had taken her closer to her dream.

As they walked towards their homes, with Aakaash pulling his strolley bag and Tiasha munching on the chocolate and hearing the details of the event, they passed the road which they had walked the most on. Since teenagers coming back from college to adults *(slightly doubtful in case of Tiasha though, but anyhow...)* discussing careers, they definitely had walked a long way together.

Parallel to where they walked were the shops which had been standing firm since the last decade. The little shop in a crowded market which sold Archies goods was running only because Tiasha liked buying 'cute' little things. The barbeque on the second floor ran because she loved paneer tikka. The aunty who sold some wonderful and classy kurtis waved at them smiling broadly, and the *chaat wala* nodded his head, greeting two of his favourite customers.

As he dropped the *aloo tikkis* into the extremely hot oil, the aroma of fried potatoes filled the ambience of Mayur Vihar, where Aakaash and Tiasha lived.

Remember the aroma I was talking about? Yes, this is it. In fact, while walking back home, there is a chaat wala who makes delicious aloo tikkis. The aroma of the tikki forces me to get some packed – every-single-time.

So, as they walked past and saw the boiled potatoes frying on the black *tawa,* Tiasha looked at them with her tummy asking her to eat and her brain instructing her tummy not to.

Just as Sonu, the owner of that chaat house added the red chutney and curd over the tikki, it started looking even more appetizing. When he sprinkled spices onto it, it looked divine, and when he finally decorated it with coriander leaves and pomegranates, Tiasha just couldn't resist. She walked towards him and said, "*Ek plate mast si tikki bana do, bhaiya.*"

She walked towards the benches and Aakaash followed. Tiasha asked, "Go on, tell me everything that happened there. Each and every little detail, mind you!"

When my mum used to come back from college when I was a kid, (which I still am, but I am talking of when I literally was) I would throw trillions of questions at her about how her day at college had been and what new development had happened and who did what and how she handled the situations and this and that. I had to know each and every detail of her workplace, the way now I come and share each and every detail of my office with her! Hah, I can keep going if not given a filter. Anyhow...

Tiasha was just as curious. Aakaash smiled at her curiosity and continued, "I was so freaked out before the show started. I felt no one would bother to attend a stand up session by an unknown comedian. I was so apprehensive. I lacked the positivity that I usually have. In fact, for the first thirty seconds, I wasn't me on stage. I was a nervous kid, looking for some inspiration. And then, I saw the number of students who had come to hear me..."

As he continued, Sonu brought out the deliciously unhealthy aloo tikkis. They were piping hot and with the wind blowing swiftly in the month of October, they looked irresistible. Tiasha kept them on the green bench of their society and heard Aakaash with pin drop silence. He was the only person she gave more importance than food.

Looking at her eyes intently set on him, he continued, "The college's auditorium was jam-packed with more than one seventy students and that became my inspiration to start. Imagine – a hundred and seventy people wanting to listen to what I had to say. The feeling in itself was unique, Tiasha. And then as I came up with my first joke, they laughed. When their laughter reached my ears, it became my reason to continue till I finished with each face sitting in the audience having a content expression. Their expressions suggested they had got more than what they expected and that expression reassured the comedian in me of his jokes."

Tiasha's smile was growing wider with every detail he added and the excitement passed on to him too. He said animatedly, "*Bas fir kya tha.* I walked down the stage as a winner…not only for the audience but for myself too."

Aakaash's voice had a decent amount of huskiness, but a major amount of deliberation to achieve his dream. His eyes, as I said, looked so tranquil that they could give shelter to a hundred refugees. Even in his early twenties, he carried the maturity that someone a decade older to him would crave. In fact, at twenty, he knew exactly what he wanted to become – different.

Being a literature graduate, I really couldn't stop myself from making a reference here – Robert Frost. I am sure you remember "The Road Not Taken?" A lot of people, including myself, want to take the road which is less travelled on. And if you are one, trust me, you will take that road…just let yourself adapt to being imperfect. Because risk takers never seek perfection as perfection needs you to settle. The greener the road, the tougher the way and the haphazard the schedules!

A lot of people want to do things differently, they have the zeal as well, but are unaware of what they really want to do. Unlike them, Aakaash knew how to be different. He knew that his satires could reach people through his jokes. Secretly, every comedian knows that his jokes are not just jokes, they are an impact which they could make on people and their ideologies. Such was Aakaash as well. Howsoever funny his jokes might seem to his friends and audience, he was an extremely sombre person personally. Except for when he was with Tiasha, because then, he forgot what common sense was. *Some people just make you build a different version of your personality. It happens! Especially when you admire a person, the way they behave becomes your way of handling situations. Ever happened with you?*

She broke a piece of tikki and while putting it in front of his mouth, she replied, "I always knew you would be the best because even you know that you are. It's just that you refuse to believe it sometimes."

Tiasha loved to make him eat with her hands; that was her right on Aakaash, she believed. If you were someone like me, you would have perhaps thought of Tiasha to be of caring sorts, who was religiously concerned for Aakaash. Well, let me tell you, both of us are wrong. The last word I would use to describe her would be caring. A better phrase probably could be impulsively emotional. She would always express what she wanted to – when she felt like cuddling her buddy, she would do that; when she felt like slapping him, she would do that too. No second thoughts and no filters!

She was a little kid, who would behave the way she wanted to. Luckily, she had a companion who would accept every tantrum of hers, without asking her to change even a bit! Friends are supposed to do that, isn't it?

Also, with a few people, we all choose to behave differently. *An example of which is from your author's life. You know, at times when work takes a toll and when writing goes missing from the day, I become extremely moody. At that time, I wouldn't speak much, but would just take all my frustration out on the best friends I have. I know I trouble them too much, but then, they love me for me being myself – a cribbing, argumentative, rotlu, irritating Devanshi. But they still choose to stay beside me, right?*

While travelling in the Metro a few days back, one of my colleagues made a pretty interesting point. He said, people always have choices and if they choose to be your friend, they accept you the way you are. If they were unhappy with you, they would have left.

If they let you stay in their friend list and let you post your thoughts on the wall of their lives, needless to say, they love you for you being you.

Digressed too much, is it?

Returning back...

Aakaash, while eating from her hands, replied, "You know that I believe in whatever you say, Tiasha." He smiled as he got a paper napkin for her and wiping the red cutney from her chubby cheeks, he adorably pinched them.

"Howsoever idiotic you look, you have the cutest cheeks any girl could have," he said.

"Which means, you notice girls' cheeks! Now that is creepy," she joked.

As they spoke, sitting cross-legged on the bench with the aroma of food lingering in their minds, they saw uncles and aunties queing in front of the Mother Dairy shop to get milk and curd, holding their milk containers. There were many groups of uncles and aunties sitting and discussing their whereabouts and remembering the good old days that they had spent.

Old age teaches you a lot. Not because of the age, but because elders have seen life much more than you have. Experience speaks, after all!

And the fact that we'd be there in a few sixty-seventy years makes it all the more interesting to listen to the experiences and memories of the elders. None of them are ignorant. They like observing things.

Just yesterday, when I boarded the Metro from Huda City Centre, I rushed inside the Metro with the wave of people who ran to grab a seat. The Metro commences from Huda and therefore, normally some efforts could land you in a comfortable seat.

While I don't really mind standing and travelling or even offering my seat to someone who needs it more, I found sitting down more comfortable to write. So I quickly took a seat in the corner of the compartment.

While I took out my laptop and waited for it to start, an uncle, who sat on the seat nearby looked at me and smiled. He commented in a nostalgic tone, "Aajkal bohut mehnat karni padti hai bachcho tumhe."

I replied, "Bilkul bhi nahi, Uncle. You used to work equally hard. It's just that times have brought technology which we can carry everywhere."

He was so happy to hear what I said. I knew he thought similarly and just wanted an acknowledgment. One sentence of mine brought a sense of pride and happiness for him. Itna toh banta hai boss.

Similarly, every time Tiasha saw groups of uncles and aunties, she would wave to them or would give them a dazzling smile, no matter how frustrated she was.

As she kept meeting and greeting new people, her house came.

Aakaash stood in front of his house, while she unlocked hers.

Being truly Indian, here I'll introduce their families. Aakaash's family included his favourite grandparents, his absolute non-favourites – his parents, a younger sister who loved him more than she loved anyone, and Tiasha, who stayed next door. They lived in the DDA apartments which were built fifty years back and therefore, did not have lifts. Staying on the fourth floor, there were two apartments facing each other – one was Tiasha's, where she stayed alone and the other was of the Kapoors', where Aakaash stayed.

Tiasha's parents' investment for her education was the reason they had purchased a house for her in one of the safest localities of Delhi. They did not want her to stay in the clustered campus PGs and find herself lost amidst the crowd. They knew she wouldn't be able to. They would rather prefer her stay at a place which was open and free; they knew the house that she was living in would be apt for her!

Her parents lived in Ahmedabad, where she was born and brought up, but she wanted to get a degree from Delhi University. High aims were always her priority. So, here she was.

Unlike everyone who finds *chachas* and *mamas* in a city to take care of their kids, her parents preferred to get her an independent house. Anyhow, little did they know that the family which stayed next door would become hers very soon. Aakaash turned out to get admission in the same college where she was, though in a different course. And since then, they had become inseparable.

Cutting the long story short, as they climbed up to the fourth floor, Tiasha ended up huffing and puffing, while Aakaash was as normal as he could be. He joked, while pressing the doorbell to his house, "Should you want, I could get you more junk food, ma'am. Some more aloo tikkis!"

Tiasha gave him a disgusted look while opening her metal door. Just then Aakaash's grandfather opened the door.

He exclaimed, "Here comes my boy. *Kaisa tha* event?"

As Aakaash narrated his experience, he walked inside his house, which smelled of his favourite *bhindi* that his granny must have cooked for him, he thought. He saw his mom busy on her laptop and his dad reading some files from his office. He thanked god they were busy, else they'd be busy trying to find faults in him.

Vaishnavi, his sister was studying in her room and everything was as monotonous as it could be for him. He felt that he had entered a world which he critiqued on stage – stereotypical and boring.

"Welcome to the same old life, Aakaash," he sighed as he spoke to his grandparents.

♌

Tiasha entered her flat in a cheerful mood. Swaying her sling bag in the air and throwing the lock on the bed, as she usually did, she opened her laptop and spoke to the two people without whom her life wouldn't be – her parents. One thousand and sixty three kilometres might be a figure that separated them technically, but each conversation, each text message that she sent, and each video call every day would diminish all those gigantic figures and would cover the distance easily.

I too stay away from my parents and yes, it becomes difficult at times. The nostalgia, the live love. But, you know what? Distance distance lagta nahi hai. In fact, whatever is happening with me, be it a tough day at work or a new crush, the first people who would know about it are my parents. Itna pakati hun na unko main din bhar. They would know each character appearing in my life!

All I can say is, Tiasha! I connect with you, darling.

After the call, she entered her kitchen, the most well-furnished place of the house and cooked for herself, because that is all she wanted to do in her life.

While cutting vegetables, she wondered how much life was like the aloo tikki that she cherished. Like a bland boiled potato, life comes to you simply. Delicious tikkis depend on the hard work of the chef, exactly like life depends on the zeal we put into life to decorate it with success.

Mehnat itni karo ki life ka swaad tikki ki tarah ho jaaye!

Thinking so, she went in for a shower, her French beans waiting for her.

Keep it simple, silly!

Unwrapping her wet hair from the towel and wiping the water droplets from her face, Tiasha walked towards her spacious balcony, from where she loved to observe the moonlight shadowing the roads. She lit a cigarette and inhaled the first drag. I don't know if I should add a disclaimer of 'Smoking is injurious to health' here. Assuming that the reader isn't as dumb as Tiasha, I believe we could proceed. No disclaimer could protect you; only your brain can. Because had disclaimers been protecting us, each cigarette pack would have saved you from smoking!

While Tiasha was smoking, the door bell rang.

She immediately sulked, wondering who could disrupt her peaceful privacy. She knew it must be Aakaash and knowing the fact that if he saw her smoking, he would have a lecture handy for her, she threw the cigarette away. She was in no mood to be lectured.

Walking towards the door and opening it, Tiasha expected Aakaash with more stories of his event. But as soon as she opened the door, he walked inside her house and broke down. He helplessly fell on the couch and cried like a little baby. Tiasha didn't know what to make of the situation and just looked at him with weird expressions. 'He was extremely happy a moment ago. What happened then?' she wondered. Then, she took a second and calmed herself first, after which, she sat next to him wrapping him in her embrace and gave him a tight hug.

No questions, no explanations, no words, only silence prevailed. He felt vulnerable to emotions, he felt helpless deep inside him. He felt weak.

Aakaash held her tightly, not wanting to leave the soft embrace. For a moment, he felt secured and protected.

Tiasha knew his tumultuous feelings, she knew his weaker side. She knew him. She stroked her hands over his back, calming him down. She knew it was rare when she would be the one acting mature, but she also knew that if Aakaash was perturbed, only she could pacify him. *Imagine peace being at conflict with itself!*

If I zoomed out the camera here, you would see Aakaash, dressed in his casuals, leaning his head on his best friend's shoulders and holding her tightly, as if leaving her would empty him of assurance. Tiasha sat like a rock with him, holding his emotions firmly and silently telling him that whatever the problem was, they'd find a solution to it.

♌

Ten minutes passed, twenty minutes passed – no questions, no answers. Just the two of them in Tiasha's drawing room, acknowledging that even when the whole world went against them, they would stay together.

Some feelings are best expressed in silence, amidst emotions. Words, at times, are spoilers.

Just then, Aakaash said, "What if my dream is not destined for me?" Helplessness poured from his voice.

Tiasha hated to see him in such a vulnerable condition. She missed the smirk on his face and the sarcasm in his speech. She never liked to see him that weak. However, keeping her likes and dislikes aside, she replied with extreme confidence in her eyes, "Why on earth would that ever happen?"

Aakaash continued, "Look Tiasha, we are not kids anymore. We are in the final year of college and soon companies will come to our college for placements with lucrative packages. You know my family well. Mom and dad pray day and night that I get a good job, regardless of the fact whether I want it or not, regardless of my wishes and my choices. What if their prayers become more effective than my dream?"

'His dreams could make him take the strongest and the weakest decisions,' she thought.

After hearing him out, she started, "I don't think that would ever happen. I know your conviction and I know their prayers too. Their prayers entail to a well-paid job, which they think you deserve. They aren't wrong either, Aakaash. But, neither are you wrong. Your dream of becoming a celebrated stand-up comedian is just more than any prayer. I am sure no company would snatch that from you because you live in that dream and that dream is your shelter."

Tiasha smiled at him as she said so. Aakaash looked visibly relaxed and replied, "Didn't you read the mail from the Placement Cell? Apticon Solutions, the leading advertising giant is coming for placements on the 28th of this month. I don't want to register, Tiyu. But, I know I will have to. Like every fucking time, I will have to do things to please my parents. And this is the worst part – 'have to'. Why can't we just do things that we want to?"

Tiasha replied softly but firmly, "Who's stopping you to do things that you want to?"

Aakaash looked into her eyes for a millisecond.

She continued after a silent moment, "Look, register for the interviews, appear for them and get the experience for your next stand-up session. *Tu mujhe dekh ke kuchh jokes hi bana lena.*

Observations make your comedy stronger; didn't you tell me this?"

Aakaash looked at her blankly for another millisecond. Then, he said, "For a change, you make sense. I can always not tell my parents that I got a job. And, one or two interviews would be good enough an experience. You are intelligent."

As he found the solutions to his webbed thoughts, he gave Tiasha a tight hug. The face which had been gloomy, now became bright. His tranquil eyes redeemed their peace and his thoughts once again, became clearer.

However, just as he hugged his best friend, he realised the lingering smell of smoke. He immediately parted and asked authoritatively, "Were you smoking again? What the hell is wrong with you Tiasha?"

Aakaash did what he would always do – lectured her – and Tiasha did what she would always do – blissfully ignored his lecture. She got up and from inside her room got her laptop. Opening the placement cell's registrations, she registered for both of them.

She could really be an irritating and ignorant friend, he thought. But, she could also be the sweetest confidant, he realised and smiled. He knew explaining it to her was useless. She would do what she wanted to, every time, till she wanted to change. He looked annoyed at this habit of hers but had no option than to let her be. He asked, as he saw Tiasha filling the form, "If you get selected, will you take up the job?"

Tiasha looked at him blankly.

They were both on the same page; they were both among many who were on the same page. After class tenth, the stress is to take up a subject stream, after twelfth it is to chose a college and score high to be among the best, and once the three fairy-tailish years of college pass, the dilemma is whether to study further – well, if yes, then get into the merit race again, or to take up placements.

However, no one can escape these. Definitely, every person who goes through this phase faces extreme dilemmas, mood swings, terrible existential crises, to name a few. But at the end of the day, you are what you choose to be. Nothing or no one else but our choices make us.

And, just when I say that, remember not always does a dress that you buy suits you well. At times, you just don't fit into it properly. *It happens.* And you should let it happen. Just remember to still choose what your heart suggests and be accountable for what you choose.

Zindagi sort ho jaani hai phir.

Being confused is alright; it helps you know which choice was closer to you when you chose it!

Chal

Next morning, when Aakaash was still asleep in the living room of Tiasha's house, she slyly opened the door and sneaked out to Aakaash's house. She quickly called his grandpa, one of the coolest people around.

"Dadu, I need some help," she whispered. He opened the door, and handed over a bag to Tiasha. Tiasha gave him a hug as she left.

Coming back to her house, she got a chilled glass of water and brought it to the living room. The next minute, she threw the glass of water on Aakaash's face, waking him up with a bright cunning smile.

"What the hell! You idiot. Tiasha, I will kill you!" he shouted.

"Do that later. For now, I need your help. So, go and get dressed. I am waiting for you in the car downstairs."

Saying this, she picked up the two bags she had kept near the door and ran down the staircase. Aakaash just looked at her with astonishment. 'How could someone be so impulsive?' he wondered. In fact, he always saw a kid inside Tiasha. It was perhaps only that child-like nature that made her what she was to him, he thought as he got up and walked towards his house to take a shower. Just then, he saw his clothes kept systematically on the table. Tiasha had taken out her favourite colours for him, as she always did.

He smiled at how she could be both ignorant, yet caring. He knew this was something exclusively for him. As he got ready, he saw Tiasha dusting her car.

A navy blue SUV that stayed safe with her in Delhi. Aakaash's family would always take care of her car's needs too. Strangely, she had a bond with everyone in his house. Even when she was stubborn, obnoxious and non-stereotypical, and surprisingly, his parents still adored her.

As Aakaash came down with his cell phone in his hand, his sunglasses looking elegant on him, Tiasha almost checked him out. She said, "You look pretty hot in dark blue, just like my SUV."

Aakaash laughed at her bad sense of humour right in the morning and asked, "What happened? Where are we going?"

Tiasha did not reply as she started her car and raced it to full speed. I believe even she didn't know where they were going, but at times, aren't unplanned trips fun to have? Especially in the situation that these guys were in, hopping off to an unplanned vacation made so much sense.

For me, unplanned visits are just till Connaught Place or farthest till Gurgaon. That's the definition of an unplanned trip for me, unlike other fancy ideas. So, just when you were envious of Tiasha and Aakaash, trust me, we are on the same level of envy.

ᔑ

They had been driving for more than five hours now, towards the heavenly state of Himachal Pradesh. Aakaash said, "You know, for no good reason, I am enjoying this moment."

Tiasha smiled as she grooved to the *dhinchak* Bollywood songs while driving. She replied, "That is because of the companion, you idiot. Also, just pass me some biscuits from the bag. I baked some last night."

Aakaash asked astonished, "Last night? I slept around two. You baked cookies after that? I am sure I annoyed you with my negativity, didn't I?"

Knowing that she cooked to de-stress herself of emotions, he could easily guess that the previous day had been a heavy day for her as well. Whenever Tiasha couldn't handle her emotions, she cooked, he knew.

However, she interrupted him and said firmly, "Give me food. I need to eat, you fool!"

As Aakaash turned towards the back seat to look for the biscuits in her bag, Tiasha looked at him from the corner of her eyes and said, "Trust me Aakaash, turn back fast, else you really look very hot today. You never know, I might fall in love with your looks!"

She laughed. He blushed.

Aakaash knew that at times, when Tiasha was in a brilliant mood, she spoke sheer nonsense and whatever she said made little or no sense at all and therefore, he peacefully ignored it. However, just while turning back, he saw the packet of cigarettes in her bag, which he picked up and threw out of the window at once. Well, only he had the daring to do so because only he could keep her calm without her cigarettes.

Tiasha simply gave him a disgusted look and this time, Aakaash peacefully ignored it with a smirk. It was more like, '*tit for tat, bro*'!

After the silent war of expressions, Aakaash opened the box of cookies and feeding her some while she focussed on driving, he said, "Your lips would turn grey. They really look beautiful as they are now. So, just stop—"

Tiasha interrupted him again, "Can we be less dramatic, please?"

When she said so, Aakaash went quiet. He simply took out his phone and checked his mailbox. He always turned to his phone when he felt the situation wasn't ideal for him to react. He compressed his emotions in that little box of technology. This time, when he was looking at it, he jumped with excitement as he read aloud:

Mr Aakaash, We would love to have you in our college as part of the cultural festival in November. Please find the details attached.

Please respond with a confirmation and a tentative date whenever we could host you!

Thanks Sir,

Hansraj College

Tiasha pressed the brakes with a jerk. With the car running on the highway at a speed of ninety, the pressing of the brakes so hard resulted in quite a jerk. She exclaimed and said, "We've just started on this trip and look, we have something to be glad about."

Aakaash smiled broadly as he thanked her for being with him. He knew howsoever impulsive and crazy she was, at the end, it was her positive attitude for his dream that kept him pumped up.

He didn't say anything, else she would cut him mid-way, telling him how typical he was. But, to himself he said, 'Her positivity brings life to my thoughts. I really wish that this friendship stays on forever. That we stay together.'

Well, he was right, if he said this out loud, Tiasha would throw him out of her car due to his melodrama.

He was looking out of the window when he noticed some momo sellers on the roadside. He looked at Tiasha and said, "There are so many people selling momos here. We should try some chicken momos."

Tiasha replied, "Yes, original momos *ka ghar toh yahin hai,* after all. We'll have many and then I'll try many more when we go back." She winked.

Aakaash said, being philosophical, "You like talking about food day and night. In this college's event, I'll speak only about food and you."

"Why the hell will you do that?" Tiasha said, with some pathetic expressions.

"Because, I think momos are like you.

Just like momos are served with mayonnaise and red sizzling chilli chutney, you too have two completely opposite sides. Sometimes you'll stay as soothing as the mayonnaise and on some days, you'll just become the unpredictable chilli chutney. *Bhaiya, ladkiyo ka samajh hi nahi aata.*"

Tiasha laughed as she commented, "That's generalisation, Mr Comedian."

And their never-ending conversation ended never!

♌

Driving through Ambala, Chandigarh, Mandi and Larji, they finally reached the most beautiful valley of Himachal Pradesh – Tirthan. Having driven for more than twelve hours, Tiasha was supposed to be tired and stressed, but somehow, she looked the exact opposite – extremely fresh and excited looking at the valley.

Aakaash looked equally elated looking around. As they hopped out of the car and saw the hills, which they had travelled with for a few kilometres, Tiasha's smile broadened till her ears. She looked so excited. She turned to Aakaash, held his hand and brought him to see the mist and cotton-like clouds.

She excitedly said, "A travel site mentioned it was a trip to heaven. It looks like one, doesn't it?"

She turned towards him and saw his serene smile. If she got an adrenal rush looking at those cloudy mountains and rivers, he saw tranquillity in them. If she grasped the tameless nature of the river, he appreciated the serenity and peace in those splashes of water. They both saw the same things, though with a different perspective.

They were hardly three kilometres away from the Great Himalayan National Park, but just being in the lap of Himalayas gave them much excitement. Looking at the cloud-covered mountains, they realised how pure nature can be. As the cool breeze brushed past their faces, they stepped closer to themselves. As the sound of water splashed into their ears, they knew themselves an inch better. As they walked alongside the river, keeping all their emotional baggage in their tent, they felt closer to life – their aims looked clearer. It seemed as if all the polluted thoughts surrounding their brain were wiped off with this purity. Everything looked sorted, all of a sudden.

No doubt, hills are so fantacized about.

It was as serene and as beautiful as a mind would be when it achieves what it wants to. Ever wondered, how when we do what we want to, we are elated and calm. But the moment we start sacrificing our choices for the choices that society wants us to make, life starts becoming complicated.

Anyway, not preaching too much, if we zoomed in to the picture at this moment, Aakaash and Tiasha's faces were glowing. They walked, ran, danced around the river, splashed water on each other and jumped in the water, clicked hundreds of selfies and took so many pictures. Their faces didn't have an iota of tiredness. Their faces beamed with joy – the joy of being free, the joy of just breaking all chains to be themselves.

As they retired to their tent in the evening after having a sumptuous dinner at the camp site, Aakaash said, "You complete me, Tiasha."

Tiasha smiled as she joked, "Why does that sound like a typical Bollywood hero, Aakaash?"

He knew the exact answer which he would get. He gave her the 'I knew this was coming' look and turning his back to her, slept. On the other hand, Tiasha scrolled through her mailbox, saw a few food recipes of the hills and came across *ghevar,* the patent sweet of the hills. While she read the recipe, she was mesmerized by just looking at the dish.

She scrolled for more images of ghevar and felt tempted. With a disc-shaped base, brownish in colour and soaked in sugar syrup, it looked deliciously heavy. So many dry fruits caressing the base decorated it beautifully. Tiasha wondered if she could use the whipping cream to add to the base; she thought it would reduce the sweetness for those who prefer light sweets and at the same time would give a continental touch to the otherwise traditional preparation.

She wrote that down in her notepad and added 'To Be Tried'.

Fantasizing about ghevar and the possibilities to modernize it, she fell asleep too.

ᔕ

The next day was spent crossing rivers, climbing rocks and fishing near the river valley. While they drove back, Aakaash was more excited. He looked completely rejuvenated, refreshed and full of enthusiasm. He was going through the pictures they had clicked and while scrolling through each picture, he narrated what the picture was about.

This happens with us, haina? Whenever we are excited, everything related to that excitement gets attached to us emotionally. Whenever I get a good review about our book, I am the first one calling my parents and sharing the screenshot of the review. It's just the excitement that I feel needs to multiply with everyone knowing of it! As my Metro buddy says, 'Mujhe toh bina piye hi chadhi rehti hai.'

Tiasha drove sincerely while listening to all the chatter of this stand up comedian.

She was happy to have him back. Perhaps that was the sole purpose of getting him out of his monotonous life. While looking at the pictures which were taken when they were crossing a river, Aakaash said, "Look at this one. I am going to post this picture with the caption, 'Super girls are scared too!'.

He laughed aloud. Tiasha punched him on his right shoulder as she sheepishly smiled looking at herself being so scared while they were crossing the river. She tried her best to retain her swag, but her efforts went in vain.

The adventure had been risky. There was cold water and it was like hanging upside down from a rope over the river. *We all get scared while crossing tumultuous rivers, don't we?*

It is altogether another argument that Tiasha looked satisfied after having crossed the river. After all, tumultuous times bring you closer to your potential.

Apticon Solutions Pvt. Ltd.

When college ends, problems begin.
'*What will I do after college?*'
'*Further studies or a job...what should I pick up?*'
'*What if I don't clear the entrances?*'

More often than not, we all have passed through that phase and have asked ourselves these questions. The last semester of college does that to you. You exactly know very well that the last exam is the easiest, because after that, life would be the examiner and life, my friend, is not a lenient evaluator.

And in such situations, what if India's leading advertising company knocks on your door, giving you a ten-lakh package with a good job. What would you do? You'd at least give it a try, wouldn't you?

Aakaash, Tiasha along with the other one seventy students of their college were trying their luck for the same.

Apticon Solutions, India's second best advertising firm had held placements in the last week of October and with a whooping package of ten lakhs, they were successful in attracting most of the students on the day of interview. Everyone thinks, *ek baar de ke toh dekh hi lete hai. Aur kuchh nahi toh experience toh mil hi jaega!*

The team who came to take the interviews arrived at nine in the morning. They knew that the turnout would be extensive. Being in the industry for more than two decades, Apticon rightfully knew how to touch the nerves of the youngsters – they paid them well and extracted the best out of the lot. With a team of seven interviewers and two HRs, they were extremely professional and systematic.

To sieve the lot of hundred and seventy five students, they first held a written test, which asked them to create a fifty-word advertisement for a pair of heels. After evaluating those entries, they finally picked seventeen students for the interview.

It was strange when they announced the names to the students. Some of them were genuinely needy of a job, yet didn't qualify, and some of them were casual – the likes of Tiasha and Aakaash – and were selected. *This is the time in college when you feel most competitive.* Maybe not competitive, but ambitious. Placements do something to you; *what* they do is a question worth asking, though.

Anyway…

The first one to enter the interview room, with all seven eyes on her, was Tiasha Shah. Walking with grace, wearing a peach sleeveless top with formal straight pants, she expressed modesty in each step that she took. Her mid-length hair waved freely, without any restriction of being tied into a formal bun. Her eyes were wide and they had no kohl or mascara, but the confidence and dreams that lined them were sparkling. *Just that they looked too tumultuous.* She was never at peace! *Restless was the word.*

Smiling throughout from where the HR representative walked her through, Tiasha was someone who made a statement as she walked and sat confidently in front of the interviewers.

"So, hi Tiasha."

The lady in a white kurta said. Tiasha liked her instantly. She replied with a smile, "It's good to be here."

The lady introduced herself, saying, "I am Naina. We've conversed over emails."

Tiasha replied, "Of course. Glad to meet you in person, Naina."

Naina looked impressed. Tiasha had a very impressive personality. When she was confident, she was beaming with surety. That surety impressed Naina. She personally loved Tiasha just after interacting with her for a while.

While questioning her, Naina asked, "Your resume says that you aim to become a chef?"

Tiasha looked self-assured as she replied, "Yes. I aim to become the top-most chef in the country and open my own restaurant."

The other interviewers certainly seemed impressed by her when she said so. However, Naina questioned, "Why do you want this job then?"

"Because, frankly I feel I need experience to make a business. Managing people and handling them make a startup work. I want to learn that."

Naina heard her carefully, after which she said, "And why do you think we should select you?"

The typical interview question, no?

Tiasha replied in a nano-second, saying, "Because of no other reason, but because I deserve it."

Naina smiled. *Wasn't that answer like the one an actor would give in a Rin ad?*

Concluding their conversation, Naina mentioned as she saw Tiasha get up and leave. She said, "Tiasha, wait a minute."

She got up and walked with Tiasha as she walked outside the interview room, stealing out time to talk to her personally.

"Yes?" Tiasha quipped with a smile. She was a curious kid, Naina thought.

"I just wanted to tell you something. You have a dream in your eyes. But, do you have a goal in your mind?"

Tiasha looked at her blankly. Yes, she knew she wanted to become a chef, but did she have a plan in place to implement her dream, she wondered as Naina continued, "I see a sharp zeal to achieve your dream, an optimistic approach too, but somewhere I lack to observe the plan to achieve that dream. In case you get the job, my suggestion would be that you take it. It will buy you time to sort your ambitions. Maybe, being the startup owner takes a struggle? I would say take that struggle."

Every word that Naina said was important to Tiasha. She was listening very carefully and she knew that these words wouldn't fade off her mind. It was one of those messages which you always want to keep safe in your phone.

As Naina concluded, Tiasha smiled and left the interview room with plenty of questions brewing in her mind.

♌

"You'll have fun inside," she told Aakaash as he walked inside the interview room. Dressed in a simple light blue t-shirt, which by the way was his patent dress, and a casual pair of jeans, Aakaash looked most disinterested, but the fact that it might give him a gag for his next stand-up event, he was excited. Adjusting his hair a bit, he eventually looked just fine to appear for an interview.

His interview went on for forty-eight minutes and perhaps he was the first candidate for whom the interviewers didn't prefer discussing job schedules and culture. Aakaash was too interesting for them to talk about work, after all. *That was the zeal one should have for his dream!*

He was too quirky to be ignored. His answers left the interviewers laughing out loud. Aakaash loved the feeling when he saw people laughing to his joke. The sound of their laughter was his appreciation.

However, the interviewers looked confused at the end of the interview. They didn't know how to react to such a candidate, who was least interested in their job but was overflowing with potential.

His answers were brutally honest and satirical. For every simple question, he had an extremely complicated answer and then a joke to simplify that complication.

Varun, an interviewer, who seemed extremely impressed with Aakaash, asked, "Given a chance, what would you choose – the job or your stand up career?"

Aakaash replied, with a spark in his eyes, "I do stand up to critique what I don't like. If I got your job, my middle class family would be the happiest and I might enjoy the salary that I would receive at the end of each month, but the stand-up comedian in me would suffocate, following rules. So, for me, it's my stand-up career."

With that, he definitely won all the seven hearts immediately and walking out, he won his heart too.

Comedians are the strangest of all, and the smartest – they would joke all day, hilariously would light up events, but in reality, I believe they are the toughest critiques of all. Never would they let go of something that their heart doesn't approve of; they'd take it out in the next gag. The audience would laugh, but would end up introspecting. That's how comedians are. That's how Aakaash was.

♌

Results are tough, results are tricky and results make you anxious. And for Tiasha, who had just started smoking, it was just a new way of handling anxiety. While Aakaash was peaceful, no matter what, Tiasha was restless in the easiest of situations. He knew this fact and that was the sole reason he stayed around – *just to be with her.*

She wanted to go out and smoke. As she picked her sling bag and got up to leave, Aakaash held her wrist and said, "Wait here."

Tiasha was about to jerk his hand away when the HR called Aakaash for the next round. Along with Aakaash, he called out for six more candidates, of which Tiasha wasn't one. Assuming that she wasn't selected, Tiasha gave Aakaash a tight hug and said, "I am leaving Aakaash, would see you at home."

Aakaash didn't stop her, knowing her impulses very well. He knew sportsman spirit was the last quality Tiasha would have. She felt bad about rejections, she felt dejected easily and she was offended even more easily. At that moment, he knew that letting her go would be the most comforting thing to do – to her and to him.

As the HR waited for Aakaash to enter, he ran behind Tiasha and gave her a hug, saying, "You are the best chef I know. I am sure no job could replace or prove that to anyone. Don't feel bad, this is just an interview."

Tiasha patted him and smiling, she replied, "Who's feeling bad? I am all happy and cheerful. You go."

She was neither happy nor cheerful, Aakaash knew. Yet, he walked back towards the interviewers. Tiasha, on the other hand, tiredly walked towards the Metro, struggling to make her way inside an extremely crowded Metro when her phone rang. Uninterested by looking at an unknown number, Tiasha said hello as if she had a gun on her forehead to oblige the caller.

"Hi, is this Tiasha?" the soft voice on the other end asked.

Tiasha replied, amidst a chaos of voices, "Yes. May I know who is speaking?"

That's our standard reply to anyone who calls us and asks formally about us or anyone. Isn't it? I used to say this line whenever I used to pick Mom or Dad's official calls. Secretly, I used to love getting into their professional space and it's perhaps because of attending all those calls that today, I understand professionalism a bit. (Wink)

As Tiasha spoke on the phone, a group of students who tried to gush inside the Metro hindered the gates from closing.

The voice replied, "Tiasha, you have been selected for the second round of interviews. Where are you?"

Tiasha stood between the push and pull of the crowd for a millisecond, after which she decided to do what no common man can do; she decided to go out of the Metro, which was immensely populated with tired students and office goers. *Bhaiya, ye ladki toh daring nikli.*

She pushed everyone, took some extremely disgusted looks and made many students miss their Metro, but somehow managed to rush out of the Metro and answered the waiting HR:

"I am so sorry. I thought I wasn't selected and therefore I left..."

She was sternly interrupted. "And what made you think that you were not selected?"

Tiasha was mum. The HR said, "Make it to the auditorium in the next ten minutes. Can you?"

And here, Tiasha did exactly what an employee of a corporate should do. She said, "Yes, it will be done."

Never say no, after all!

She ran through the people, picked up a cycle from the cycle stand outside the Vishvavidyala Metro station and rode through a crowded street of students. At the gate, she kept her cycle and ran at the speed of light. Each carbohydrate in her body cried as they were being killed by her passion to reach the auditorium.

At this moment, she was already an employee of Apticon, who was running. She didn't know why she was, but she was. *We rush each day, we rush each second...do we know why?*

As she reached the auditorium, she almost fainted. And this impressed the interviewers the most. Who wouldn't want an employee who could even faint to get the job? This is what every employer looks for. *I too, as an employer, would love such an employee in my company!* The interviewers got up from their seats, helped her with water and asked her if she needed to rest. They were really caring, I must say. Otherwise, all what we have seen of corporate is being brutally practical.

Being the stubborn person that she was, she replied, "If I wanted to rest, why would I take so much risk to reach here on time? We can go ahead with the interview."

Naina smiled. She knew that this girl was special and had the potential to rise up in the company. She said, "Come then."

As Tiasha walked towards the interview table, Aakaash laughed and told himself, 'This girl can mark an impression on each mind she interacts with. Tiasha, she is, after all.'

It was true. Even if unknowingly, she always became the centre of attention, and knowing her too well, he knew that she loved it.

He smiled at her, but deep inside, was slightly disturbed by the interest Tiasha had developed for the job immediately. He was concerned about the chef inside her.

Till a few days back, Tiasha wanted to sit in the interviews to get experience and exposure. She never wanted to desperately take up a job. When did she become so serious, he wondered.

Her optimism and diligence towards the job left him perturbed. He was someone who would be crystal clear about what he wanted to do with life, whereas she was someone who would take the most zig-zag way of reaching her destination.

They were both dreamers, but one would take the smooth way, while the other loved taking a bumpy roller-coaster, it seemed.

Today, he wondered why she wanted to turn destiny around? Perhaps he did not understand. Perhaps she had no answers to make him understand. Perhaps she was clueless herself. Perhaps. Yes, perhaps.

However, the Tiasha who sat for the interview now was a different person...much more confident and more convincing.

As Tiasha sat firmly and answered most questions with confidence and passion, her phone vibrated. It was her mom. Now, she finally did something which an office-goer wouldn't; she stopped the interviewers mid-way and said, "Excuse me. I have to take this call."

She excused herself, spoke to her mom and then came back to sit in front of the panel. The seven pair of eyes looked at her with mixed expressions – she was determined, yet stubborn; she was crazily passionate, yet grounded – she was a perfect match to what they were looking for, but were they the perfect match to what she wanted?

She said as she sat back, "I can run and faint, but I can't keep my mom wait in anxiety for anything…even for a job."

These best friends were true dialogue writers, it seemed. The interviewers smiled at her answer. They saw a little child in the twenty-one-year-old, and her fresh energy was contagious.

With Tiasha's interview, the second round of interviews too came to an end. Speaking of that, the final list of the students who were selected was announced by Naina.

"So, finally we've come to the end of the interviews and we all know we'll cross ways again, so no one goes home disheartened. However, the ones whom we have selected are: Arnika Das, Aakaash, and Tiasha Shah."

Announcing her name, Naina looked at her and smiled. The smile said a lot. It showed her trust in Tiasha; it showed her belief in the candidate that she had selected.

As for Aakaash, Naina said, "We almost know you'll not join, but we did not want to lose even one chance of having you in our team. Think of it Aakaash, it's not a bad option to manage both."

Tiasha smiled as she stood beside Aakaash. She knew Aakaash was adamant and determined to achieve his dreams. No one and no opportunity would take him away from his ambition in life, she knew. She also knew that he would never take the offer, even if his family needed it. *His dreams were bigger than handling responsibilities.*

Chalo, at least one of them was sensible and sorted.

ᘓ

As the Apticon team left, Aakaash and Tiasha became their normal selves.

Aakaash said, "I have talent, it seems."

Tiasha smiled as they walked down till the canteen, "Yes. Being in my company helps, you see."

Aakaash smiled as he sat on their favourite table in the canteen, just next to the food counter. Tiasha loved observing how Ravi bhaiya, the head chef of their canteen cooked various dishes. She had built a great rapport with Ravi bhaiya in the last three years.

Like every day, she walked up to the canteen counter, which was almost like a second home to her, and said, "Ravi bhaiya, chicken *ko chhod ke veg me kya hai*?"

And, here comes the biggest point of difference between the two best friends – Aakaash was a whole-hearted non-vegetarian, whereas Tiasha was a *dadi-maa* types complete vegetarian. Although she cooked the best chicken dish you could ever have, she would never taste a bite of it.

There was no conflict of thoughts; just when they became bored of life, they loved arguing! *LOL, if I can be 'cool' enough to use this. Or perhaps, LMAO. My cousins would be so proud of me, reading these 'cool' acronyms, which only they knew earlier! (Khushi ke aansu!)*

Aakaash walked up as he heard Tiasha ordering vegetarian food, and said, "Why are you boycotting my chicken, Tiasha?"

He almost got offended at the discrimination his chicken faced. He wanted to be just to all the slaughtered hens, it seemed.

Tiasha retorted, "I will not have non-vegetarian food, Aakaash."

Aakaash reverted sharply, with a kid's zeal to fight, "What do you mean? Are you an honest chef? A gourmet chef has to love everything people like to eat."

"Yeah, right. I am a chef. I should know how to cook everything, which doesn't necessarily mean I should love to eat everything as well. But, how will you understand... one needs brains to understand things, no? And oh, I forgot, you've got that missing since childhood." She gave it right back. Whenever Tiasha argued, her expressions were the cutest. And every time she looked cute, Aakaash secretly wanted to forget everything and give her a tight hug.

He wanted to do exactly the same even then.

'She really looks adorable when she argues this way,' he thought. But, bringing his lost mind to the correct track, he came to the agenda of his war and interrupted her, "Oh yes, my lost brain is hanging out with you only. That's why you know about its whereabouts so well. And you, you *toh* are the most intelligent person one could ever meet. I am so glad I can have some snacks with her highness."

"Good. You should be," Tiasha said as she turned to the counter, where by now, all the workers were having a good time laughing at them. They had witnessed such arguments almost daily in the past three years. In fact, they loved these two, because these two loved them. Especially Tiasha, who loved every chef that she met; she knew what cooking was, what feeding a starving student was.

Turning to Ravi bhaiya, she said, "*Bhaiya, aap bahar aa jao.*"

She told him she wanted to cook. Aakaash smiled at her innocence, for she did this often. Whenever she got overwhelmed with boring lectures, she would just jump inside the canteen kitchen and cook.

PS: This was breaching college rules, by the way. But, rules todna bhi toh art hai na. Sshhh. That's our secret.

He knew now she would meet herself, which perhaps she was bent on moulding to a different identity after the morning interview. He exactly knew how this girl could find the correct path, her path. *She wasn't meant to be an employee, he knew.*

Quickly adding all the tested spices and sausages, she cooked crispy chicken for her best friend. She knew he loved it. He loved every experiment Tiasha did on him, he was that sweet. He never said her food was not up to the mark. Even if he didn't like it, he ate it, for he knew he couldn't even match up to half of what she cooked. He was the best critique, who would appreciate everything while eating, but would send an email with a truthful feedback at night. Tiasha loved him for what he was for her...everything.

For herself and the vegetarian lovers, she went on to cooking Hot Chilli Potatoes with garlic naan.

As she added the potatoes in honey and sauces, she looked how they changed their colour. For a second, she feared whether her life too would change with today's decision of taking up the job, but then distracted herself by her cooking and quickly served the potatoes in four plates.

Aakaash looked at her while she cooked. He saw the most sensible version of her only then. She just looked different when she was in the kitchen. He quickly got a bottle of Coke and served it in four disposable glasses. He went on and got Ravi bhaiya, along with all the guards and others around to the table and served them the freshly cooked potatoes, chicken and Coke. At times, their thinking process went and met exactly at one point. That's what best friends are like, I guess.

After serving everyone, Tiasha and Aakaash got their plates. Aakaash proudly had his bite of chicken while Tiasha ate her chilli potatoes like a monkey would eat bananas. It was Ravi bhaiya who had made her fond of this dish. They all looked like a big, happy family! And this wasn't the first time Tiasha had cooked for everyone. In the past three years, she had cooked a thousand times for them!

And then, life too is somewhere like these chilli potatoes only – sweet with honey and success and spicy with hurdles and spices. The graph of life too, keeps flowing between these two emotions.

On that note, the day ended with these two arriving at their adjacent flats. Aakaash had warned Tiasha not to tell anyone anything at home. He knew his dad would never be able to digest that his son wasn't taking up a ten-lakh worth of job. He feared being thrown out of the house that very moment.

He ordered as they climbed up the stairs, "You dare be my Dad's puppy. Clearly say that I was rejected."

Tiasha nodded like a five-year-old kid when told not to reveal a secret. She knew that with a few things, Aakaash was strict and those things, she did as he said, obediently.

As she always did since the past three years, she kept quiet and went to bed with a happy pillow next to her.

Tiasha was basically confused. She was perturbed because she was confused, and confusion takes you nowhere. She knew she was the only one out of the three selected candidates who had signed the official contract immediately and was now bound to the company for a year. When she told her parents, they were happy for her. Any parent would be, after all. But, little did they know how impulsively she had taken the decision. She, I believe, just wanted to experiment, perhaps the best and worst trait of any chef – and her parents would never stop experimenting. After all, risks were Tiasha's best friends; she was madly in love with them. *Remember, crossing the river? (Wink)*

But, before sleeping, as it always happens, random thoughts about the future hit her head, which she was hitting back with counter-arguments continuously. Now she had anyway taken a decision and being a Salman fan, she didn't want to go back on her commitment.

The earthquake which stabilised life

The next few days were tough.

With the final exams approaching Tiasha and Aakaash at a striking speed, they were forced to thrust books upon their lives. After having a few grand farewell parties, it was extremely difficult to focus on studies, especially when they were in their '*Dil Chahta Hai*' phase of life. When we were in school, didn't we take a hell lot of time to come out of the 'bye-bye' phase and switch on the 'study mode'? *Bas, wahi ho raha tha yahan.*

Oh, by the way, both of them looked extra-ordinarily beautiful in their farewell pictures, which Aakaash was scrolling through at midnight. He was bored with books and wanted to vent out his frustration. For him, Tiasha was the only solution.

As he saw the pictures, with Tiasha giving him a Panda hug, dressed in a black sari with a golden border and a fancy deep-necked blouse, she complimented his dark black coat and jeans. He just smiled as he looked at her smile and then his smile. He knew he couldn't be happier. He knew she completed his smile.

While he looked at the pictures, his mind forced him back to reality and brought back the conversation he had had with his father during dinner.

ᔕ

"So, you mean to say all the companies have completed their recruitment?"

His dad asked, tearing a bite from his hot chapati. Aakaash, along with his family, sat next to him and served himself vegetables, daal, and chapatis. He also made some space in his plate and his mind to hear the unending lecture that was coming his way.

It is said, a family that eats together, stays together. But here, it was just the opposite. Here the scene was just the opposite. Whenever this family ate together, they argued together.

Aakaash looked up and replied wryly, "Yes. And how many times would I repeat this, Papa?"

His dad retorted, "Till the time you get a proper job. Don't tell me you couldn't even get one job out of so many?"

"Potential toh itna hai, result kyun nahi milta isko," his father thought aloud. Aakaash looked perturbed as he struggled through the continuous banter that was shot at him daily. And his only escape, his college, was no longer an escape as the preparation leaves had started.

Every day as the sun came up, Aakaash's parents would start asking him about placements and jobs, which was exactly the topic he didn't want to talk about. Doesn't that happen at times? We run from a few thoughts diligently and they run back to us even more diligently.

Anyway, his dad kept asking more questions and Aakaash kept answering them. He knew he couldn't change things, so rather had to just accept them the way they were. He was too firm to kneel down in front of these stereotypical demands of his family to get a 'defined' job. Why should he, he wondered.

He knew he had potential and he knew he could use it in a career where it was needed. He didn't need a corporate job to prove that he was worth surviving in life. He always wondered why he didn't have parents like Tiasha's. She was casual about life, she was happy go lucky and she was extremely confused. Yet her parents supported her will to become a chef with an open heart.

That night too, after the conversation on the dinner table, Aakaash was wondering while lying down on his bed about life, his choices and his career. He was, to be precise, confused about what he really wanted from life. Apparently, he was really sure about things in life but had no support from his family. At times, he just wanted to give up on a struggling career and do what his family expected; at other times he felt suffocated from within and sometimes, he just wanted to run away.

Would running away ever be a solution?

Would comedy ever give me the acclaim that I deserve?

Am I choosing the right path?

Would I make it big?

And questions like these kept popping up in his head like popcorns would pop in a cooker. With each popcorn-like thought popping to the lid of the cooker, it made a mark on his lid-like brain. And with each prick, Aakaash felt weaker. Well, this tends to happen when you have no support from those around you to achieve your dreams. This happens when parents themselves make a one-arm distance between them and their kids. This happens, but this shouldn't.

♌

On the other hand, Tiasha slept peacefully with her arms around her tan-coloured teddy bear. She had had a pretty hectic day and after reading a lot about some random technical stuff from her college books, she had gone to sleep very late.

If you zoomed in to her bedroom, you would see all the books lying around the bed, some biscuits giving her books company and her recipe booklet sleeping peacefully next to them. In between all of them, she slept with her teddy bear next to her, wrapped in her arms with the room air conditioned comfortably at 24 degrees Celsius.

♌

And when she was fast asleep with all the worry packed up in a small bag and thrown to Mars, tranquillity decided to ditch her. At 2 a.m. the land wanted to groove to a fast tune, it seemed. When everyone was fast asleep in Delhi NCR, there were waves in the ground that shook their souls.

Being an area prone to earthquakes, Delhi was used to such shocks. News channels quickly created their breaking news and started to flash the magnitude of the earthquake. It was 4.8.

Aakaash, who was still awake, quickly got up and rushed to his grandparents' room. He woke them up and asked them to rush down the stairs. The buildings seemed hassled and perturbed as everyone rushed downstairs to be saved from the feeling of being on a roller-coaster on the top floors.

After he helped his grandmom get down, he quickly rushed back to Tiasha. He knew she wouldn't even feel the strong vibrations; she slept like a sloth when she did. It was strange that even when the world wanted to save their lives and themselves from the trauma of facing the vibrations in their hearts, Aakaash didn't even think a second before rushing upstairs to the fourth floor to Tiasha.

The earthquake went on for fifty seconds, after which it was stable again just to come back for another thirty-seven seconds.

But, Tiasha slept like she hadn't slept for the last eighty years. As Aakaash called her, messaged her, rang the door bell and shouted his lungs out to wake her up, she slept as if she was drugged with chloroform.

Aakash kept calling her as the aftershocks returned, and didn't walk down until the earthquake stabilised and everyone started climbing upstairs.

Tiasha finally woke up when she heard perturbed voices of people discussing the earthquake as they climbed up. The first thing she did was to check her phone.

There were seventy missed calls from Aakaash.

She ran outside to see him standing at her door with a perturbed face. He almost thought her sleep would peacefully lead them to sleep forever with such recursive earthquakes.

Tiasha, as she opened the door, had a fat tear in her eyes, apprehensions in her mind and disappointment with herself as she saw him stand there – just for her. She didn't say anything, she didn't move, nor did she react to anything. She just stood frozen.

Aakaash looked at her fearful face, her sleepy, hassled eyes and walked inside her house, to give her a tight hug. He wrapped her in his arms in an assuring way as he said, "The earthquake has passed. Relax Tiasha."

Relax? She was nowhere near relaxing. When she had been relaxing, the whole world was shaking. Now, when the whole world was at peace, she was shaking with fear. Aakash just took a step back to get some water for her, when she held him and hugged him even more tightly. She felt extremely lucky to have him. There was an emotion which told him that no matter what happens, no matter where they go, no matter if the world turns upside down like it did today, he would never leave her. Perhaps today was the day when they realised that they were not only each other's strength, but also the biggest weakness.

ℌ

As Aakaash kept her wrapped in his embrace, Tiasha said, "I am sorry."

Aakaash stroked her hair as he replied, "There's nothing to be sorry about, Tiyu. I am here, you are here too, and luckily, both of us are alive to achieve our dreams. What's the need of this stupid sorry then?"

Tiasha sobbed fearfully.

"Thankfully the earthquake didn't affect us the way it could have. But, what if it had Aakaash? And what if you—"

She continued after a long pause, "The problem is that you are too selfless and I am too selfish. The bigger problem is that you know this, yet you want to be the selfless best friend for me. And you know what's worse? I will let you to wait for me forever and still be confused about what I want from life. I feel selfish and mean."

Aakaash heard her silently. He knew Tiasha was impulsive, had confused emotions and puzzled feelings, yet he wanted to stay with her…forever.

He replied, still holding her tightly in his embrace,

"That is fine. I have a choice, and I choose to like selfish people."

Just when she was about to reply, he said, "And now, just shut up Tiasha. You talk too much. And, by the way, why were the keys of your house not in my bag? You took them out, didn't you?"

She sobbed and smiled sheepishly, replying, "Yes, I forgot my keys in the car and took yours!"

"And who do you think is supposed to return them back to me?" he asked with a smirk.

Tiasha didn't say anything else but once again gave him a tight hug. Aakaash smiled at her innocence and took her to her room. He sat with her as she slept holding his hand close to her cheeks.

The earthquake fortunately did not damage the lifelines of Delhi. Though it was mentally exhausting, but thankfully did not affect the lives of a million people staying under the shelter of India's capital, which is an earthquake-prone zone. However, what it did was slightly tumultuous. It grew feelings inside two hearts – one easily accepted them, the other easily rejected them. And perhaps, what was always around but never felt, no longer could be ignored. Feelings were crude, emotions were immature, Tiasha was ignorant and Aakaash – well, he was, I don't know – just perhaps happy to know his feelings, or maybe disappointed with them. What he felt generally stayed with him. Little did he share about himself apart from those comedy gags.

Comedians are serious, as I always say!

To do or not to do

Exams are funny; you prepare for them, you give them all the time, you put in all the efforts to study for them to get a good score and then one day they finally end.

And all of a sudden, all the bright plans that your mind was cooking while the exams were going on, stop immediately. *When I was in school, before every exam, I used to imagine myself playing cricket, football, hanging out with friends, going to parks and movies and malls and having sleepovers with my girl gang. Purva, my childhood best friend, and I would walk in the evening before every exam, no matter how much of the syllabus was left to complete and every day would fantasize about life after exams.*

And then, the day when we'd come back from the last exam, we'd be so bored with all the plans that we made that we'd end up sulking that we had nothing to do. I'd just crib all day saying 'I was getting bored.' My Dadi would know how many times I was just whinning ranting that mere paas toh kuch kaam hi nahi hai. Main bore ho rahi hun.

Exactly like us, Aakaash and Tiasha also kept cribbing about how bored they were, except for the fact that both of them had a lot to work on. Aakaash was busy preparing for his new Vlog and Tiasha had trillions of things to think about.

She was in a dilemma whether to take up the job or not. She knew Apticon would change the way she was – it would change her lifestyle, her opinions and would give her an insight into the life beyond being carefree. She was looking forward to it because she knew it would give her a perspective to look at life and gain experience to utilise for her restaurant.

But, would it be a correct decision? her mind quipped.

And this dilemma continued for a while. Tiasha thought about her job even before she had started going to office, she spoke to her parents and to Aakaash for hours, and most times, the conclusion to each conversation would be more confusion at the end. With Tiasha, the problem was that no matter what anyone said, she wouldn't believe anything till she was extremely convinced. Normally, she took a decision very quickly, and unplanned ones too. She was someone who would always go with the flow.

For example, she wanted to become a doctor till class ten. But, when it came to filling the forms for choosing the subjects, she decided and announced to her parents that she would take humanities. Until the previous year, she thought she'd give the UPSC exams a shot. But, when Apticon came, she signed their contract for a year…that's how much she trusted her gut feeling.

She was always clear of what she was deciding, however unplanned it was, until Apticon came into the picture. Today, she felt confused, perhaps, disillusioned.

And when she was solving these puzzles, the only people she liked talking to were her parents.

"You've always chosen what you wanted to do, Tiyu. Never take a leap which will change you as a person," her dad said.

Her mom added on the Skype call, "Of course. Learn from the learning that you get from experience, but never let any learning influence your mindset."

"Plus, it is fine to make mistakes, beta. At least you should know what made you fall so that while walking ahead, you could take care of that," her dad completed.

As Tiasha listened to them, she said, "That is true. And perhaps the job would give me time to introspect, Papa. After I complete my bond period of a year, we could work more seriously on the restaurant."

Her dad nodded and said, "Just get the experience. And then, I trust you with your abilities."

Tiasha had a broad smile by the end of this conversation. Just before keeping the phone down, she exclaimed, as she remembered, "And Maa, Papa... there's some great news."

They excitedly asked about it. "What's it?"

"Didn't I mention the food magazine, *Cakes and Cuddles*?"

Cakes and Cuddles was one of the best cooking magazines of the world. They were organising a food festival in different parts of the world to explore talent in the culinary field. And the news that Tiasha wanted to share was that they were coming to India in July 2017.

She explained their festival to her parents with shining eyes, "So, I told you that I registered on their page a month back, right? Just yesterday night I received a mail from their team mentioning that they would be organising a food festival in a resort in Mahabaleshwar. There would be many workshops and they would be hosting some of world's best chefs there."

Her dad seemed excited, "Oh, that'll be fun."

Tiasha continued, "Yes Papa. In fact, they have a month-long competition too, which would have a knock out challenge daily for thirty days and out of the final fifteen, they will select the best chef."

"This is the confidence I see in your eyes when you talk about your dream, Tiasha. Apply for this," her mom said.

"The registration fee is 12,650 rupees." Tiasha said.

"Fill it up. You are not supposed to think about expenses at the moment," came the reply from the other end, which was expected. *(Wink)*

Tiasha smiled as she thanked god for gifting her with the best parents – not for the cash, but for their support. She knew she was nothing without their encouragement. She knew they were her driving force.

She said, "I will register tonight itself. They need two recipes to judge from. I was thinking..."

And her never-ending conversations ended never and she fell asleep while the video call was still on. Her parents loved to see her sleep so peacefully. I believe every parent does.

Tiasha, on the other hand, felt lighter in her heart and happier in her mind each day when she spoke to her parents, or perhaps, best friends I should say.

You know, especially when you stay away from your parents, there are many chances that the distance would become the distance between you guys, but at the same time, it's possible that the distance removes all the emotional distance that you have.

For me, when I came to Miranda House, I felt there was too much to explore in Delhi and that's precisely the only reason I love Delhi so much. When I stay away from home, in a home away from home, I feel that yes, the distance prevails in terms of kilometres, but there's nothing which is happening in my life that my parents are unaware of. It depends on the choices that we make – if we wish to reduce the distance, technology is a bridge. If we don't, nothing else can.

♌

Anyway, so as Tiasha registered for the competition in Mahabaleshwar, she gave a high-five to Aakaash, who sat next to her, looking at the comments and likes on his next YouTube update.

(He was obsessed with his fans, I am telling you.) He said, "I am happy that the audience reach has multiplied since the first video. But, there's still time in that viral break, Tiasha."

Tiasha closed the lid of her laptop and turned to him, saying, "What the hell yaar, Aakaash. Don't you think you crib too much? Twelve thousand likes and thirty-four thousand views aren't less. And this one has double the views than the previous. People are responding to your content because it is fresh. Everyone wants a break from sexist jokes, after all."

"I know, but..." he tried to speak.

"Shut up. And help me pack my bags for Jaipur," she ordered authoritatively.

♌

As she took out a white dress from her cupboard and kept it in a gigantic black suitcase, she remembered that she had worn that dress when she first participated in a cooking competition. That day when she picked up the trophy for the best chef, she knew she had to become India's best chef. There are some moments and memories in your life which you never want to let go of. *Haina?*

As she carefully placed that dress inside, she knew what she wanted in life. She smiled remembering those old memories but that smile contained an artist's disillusionment with the world, and that smile contained her dissatisfaction with the way her cooking career was shaping. *Confusion, oh confusion!*

Till the previous year, Tiasha was more than happy to take part in competitions, write new recipes, add salt to tea, add sugar to vegetables and experiment ad infinitum. But since the day she got placed, she was apprehensive of what future had in store for her. Since the last six months, she kept wondering of what she should bother about – the luminous present or the uncertain future. With many doubts and some certainty, she chose the former. She took up her job in Apticon Solutions, but every step that she took towards the company, unconsciously took her ten steps back, making her confused. Even miserable.

Personally, I have realised that being confused for a while is fine, but it leads you nowhere. Rather, take everything that comes to you with zeal to learn more. I can proudly say today that each day I work, I learn; each day I write, I try to grasp things. Problems toh aati hi hai yaar, aaengi hi. Escalations honge hi office me…but problems se darr ke toh koi fayda nahi hoga. Haan, unse seekh ke zaroor hoga! Each mistake you make could be a learning that ye repeat nahi karna hai.

Not that she was the first one taking up a job in lieu of a heartfelt hobby, but was cooking just a hobby for her? Was it *just* another career option that she had or was it her life? She was desperately looking for all these unanswered questions. We all do, at some point of time.

As of now, she kept her dresses systematically in her suitcase, trying to sort her brain of all the confusions as well. *Jo bhi hoga dekha jaega.*

Tiasha knew that she could be weak, could be confused, she could cry (though she tried not to, at least in front of the world), she could be frustrated, be full of angst, but at the end of the day, the only thing she knew wouldn't change was her love for her work. The work that her heart and soul wanted her to do.

She knew she had already discussed all of this with her parents earlier, but just a day before leaving, each apprehension made a sly way into her head.

This sounds typically dramatic, doesn't it?

As she kept her toothbrush, she added his companion, the toothpaste, with their gang of face wash, scrub and kohl, the only cosmetic she used apart from Vaseline, which kissed her lips often. While she zipped the chain of her small pouch, she tried to gather all her scattered thoughts at one place. As she was struggling with her thoughts, Aakaash entered. Calculating her expressions exactly, he said, "Relax, Jaipur would be fun. You'll come back a different person from there!"

ꝏ

Why is Tiasha ranting about Jaipur so much? Who's going to Jaipur and why? What's going on, after all?

Well, Apticon had decided to train their employees before bringing them to the working floor. They had planned a sixty-day training in their residential head office in Jaipur to brief the recruits about their profile and work culture.

It was a pretty interesting initiative by the company, especially because this was the first job for almost all the campus recruits and to update them with all the information before putting them to work was a sensible act to do. Undoubtedly, the best companies know how to get the best work. In fact, that's why they were standing strongly on the top. *Employees make a company. Satisfied employees make a successful company!*

And advertising was anyway a very competitive market. For staying at the top, you needed the best strategies. *Just yesterday, while I was speaking to my parents, I mentioned that employees make a company, just like I say readers make writers.* The companies who are able to understand their employees best, flaunt their success and those who aren't, unfortunately fall as quickly as they climb.

Apticon was in the former category, it seemed.

So, now you know where Tiasha was headed.

Part - II

As delicious as white sauce pasta

"Hey guys, welcome onboard! We'll all leave for Jaipur in the next ten minutes. Please get inside the bus."

Tiasha was about to embark on a journey she was apprehensive about. A journey which made her excited and anxious, all at the same time. A journey that she knew wouldn't be a cakewalk.

While all the campus recruits waited to leave for Jaipur, the HR guy briefed them with the rules and regulations. He said, "We've planned a good training and the residences are good too. Therefore, the only rule we'll all follow is that none of us would be able to meet anyone from outside the campus. But, trust me, you'll love the campus. We won't let you miss anyone."

Big boss big boss big boss.

This tune immediately started playing in most minds at that moment. This was perhaps the biggest hurdle that Tiasha would face. She was emotionally too connected with Aakaash and her family, and staying away from Aakaash for sixty days meant the biggest challenge for her. However, setting aside all such unwanted negative thoughts, Tiasha just focussed on the start of this journey.

'Go with the flow,' she told herself.

♌

Their bus had started from the Gurgaon office a minute ago and as they travelled on, Tiasha looked out of the window. Don't you think she, along with all the recruits, was too daring to hop on a trip which they knew very little about! *Risks change you, risks make you.*

The start wasn't that bad. It was exciting for her. Inside her mind, butterflies jumped and danced as she started on a new journey.

She excitedly posted on Facebook:

'Excited to start preparing a new dish. Started working at Apticon Solutions, Gurgaon.'

Within minutes of her departure, there were more than two hundred likes and fifty-seven comments congratulating her. Her mom commented on the status:

'I am more excited to see how this dish affects the sweetest dish of your life.'

Out of all the comments, Tiasha just replied to her mom's comment and kept her phone inside, as others in the bus kept laughing and chatting about the new trip which had just begun for them.

While Tiasha sat alone, looking outside the window and observing how the breeze swayed the trees, her life too was being swayed by a decision that she had taken over-excitedly. It could sail her through, or could sink her altogether. She just hoped the former would come true.

And just when she was talking in soliloquies, a timid looking girl said with a sugar-coated sweet voice, "Hey, I left the cap of my bottle open and it messed my seat. Do you mind if I sit next to you?"

Tiasha smiled peacefully as she replied, "Of course not, come!"

She picked up her beige handbag and kept it on her lap. The girl sitting next to her was a complete chatterbox. With the cutest expressions, she was one character who had just hopped out of Rajshree movies, it seemed. With a mellow voice, she sung all songs as everyone played Antakshari. Tiasha looked out of the window as her new friend tapped on her shoulder and said, "You also join us. Songs are lovely. They are so energetic."

Tiasha loved this girl's attitude towards life; she was extremely positive towards everything. She looked so cheerful. For a minute, Tiasha wanted to steal some bits of her attitude from her, for she herself hardly bothered about others, she was so pre-occupied with herself. *Time kaha milega baaki sabke bare me sochne ka bachchi ko?*

As Tiasha still looked lost and the girl sitting next to her got tired of singing, she turned towards her and introduced herself, saying, "I am Srishti, and I am glad to meet you. Aren't you the one who's a chef?"

Tiasha smiled and replied enthusiastically, "I am equally elated. I am Tiasha. And yes, the chef."

When she introduced herself as a chef, her eyes sparkled with confidence.

Srishti replied, "I love cooking and in these sixty days, you are going to teach me all your secret recipes. Deal?"

She extended her hand to close the deal and Tiasha happily held it. One new journey had begun, a new friend was near her, and Tiasha felt slightly less lonely, if that is how I could express the tumultuous emotions that she was going through.

It's so difficult to describe emotions at times...it's actually difficult to summarise using words how one was feeling. She was perhaps feeling two hundred things in one moment. How can anyone express such emotions, after all?

The one who could understand all those two hundred emotions in one go is the one who you could spend the rest of your life with, I believe. Sometimes, people don't say anything but they understand exactly what is going on in your mind; sometimes, they'll deliberately trouble you with their attitude so that no one else can. At times, they just scold you for being immature so that no one else could point that out.

It's rare, but at times, someone can be so giving that they take all your angst for making you a better version of yourself! If you meet some such person, forget everything and seal a deal for a lifetime! Don't be Tiasha is all I would say! (Wink)

♌

After a journey of four hours and millions of emotions, their bus stopped at the Jaipur residences. Each employee was given a single room to stay in. Their rooms weren't spacious, but it gave them space to stay alone and have them to themselves when they retired after a brainstorming innings of the day. Tiasha was fifteenth in the row when the guard handed over the keys of room number 106 to her. She signed against her name and moved with one big thirty kg black suitcase, a little black bag and her beige laptop bag clinging to her shoulder, a couple of more small bags trying to find place in her hands, and a ringing mobile phone. As Tiasha took the keys and looked around for a lift, the guard announced, "There is no lift, madam. Please take the staircase."

Two floors, no lift, almost thirty kgs of clothes and shoes – wow! Tiasha sighed. With five huge bags and a tiring journey, it wasn't something that appealed Tiasha at all. Struggling up the stairs, she finally reached her room. Room 106 – the corner-most room on the floor that looked isolated.

As Tiasha unlocked the door, her eyes checked out the room dramatically. The room didn't even have enough space for her bags, forget herself, she thought. The pale yellow walls looked plain and boring, unlike her room in Delhi. She missed her luxuries the very moment she saw the room. *Comfort zone se bahar aana itna easy bhi nahi hota, after all.*

'A new start should not have any negative cribbing.' She repeated what her mom had told her.

As this thought revolved in her mind, her lips stretched into a smile and excitedly, she started to put her clothes in the old and trite cupboards, dusting the extra dust off the shelves and replacing it with joyful excitement. The room was small, but her own. *Remember, Virginia Woolf's* A Room of One's Own?

The pampered kid was taking up responsibilities of the small room. *Never had she* dusted her room in Delhi, *never had she* wanted to decorate the room so that it looked better. But today, she did happily.

And in another two hours, the tiny room became one of the most creatively decorated rooms. With colourful stick-on notes on the pale wall, all her cosmetics on the shelf, clothes systematically folded and kept in the cupboard, a wind chime near the window and the most colourful bed sheet, the room looked lively.

See how positivity can transform a pale wall to a colourful one, white bed sheets to colour-splashed ones and a de-motivated Tiasha to an enthusiastic one.

After putting everything in place, Tiasha stood at the door and took a video of the room to send it to Aakaash. She quickly changed into a comfortable lower and was looking for a t-shirt to wear when she realised that there was something special for her – it was Aakaash's favourite sky blue t-shirt, which he wore during most of his stand-up events. He had slyly put it in her bag and had drawn a smiley on the right corner. A note which was hidden inside the t-shirt read,

It's a new journey, but my Tiasha will go through this. Howsoever cliché you may want to define my gestures to be, I'd always be your cliché best friend. Keep smiling like the smiley. (I know this is old but, deal with it! I couldn't get anything better.) And, if staying alone is tough for you, staying without you is the worst punishment someone could give me too. So, with this sadistic approach, be happy, you idiot!

Tiasha smiled when she read this note. She immediately dialled Aakaash's number. Aakaash exclaimed as he picked up her phone excitedly, "Has Jaipur seen the worst of you already, or is it yet to come?"

Tiasha laughed and replied, "Not yet. It has just seen the happy me. Climax stays for the end."

Aakaash smiled on hearing her voice. In a few years, he had forgotten how life was without her. All he knew was that she was his only family who understood him. And being alone in her house was a bane, he thought. It had just been a day, but his life looked empty to him.

In fact, staying away from her was secreting strange feelings in his mind. When they had been together, they never got time to think about anything else, but about each other and their careers. But now, when they were separated by distance and Aakaash had an empty mind and plenty of time, feelings were popping up inside his little brain.

As they spoke, Tiasha sensed the sad vibes on phone when no one spoke for a minute. She said, "Accha, all this apart, when are you uploading your next Vlog?"

"Not yet. I was planning to first—" he spoke when he was abruptly interrupted:

"Why am I hearing, 'not yet'? I told you that the only way to crack the internet is to be diligent and stubborn. I don't want to hear anything else. You have a lot of time now, sit in my place, clean it every day and prepare for your video. Mind you, just don't mess with my kitchen."

Her voice sounded firm and extremely confident. Funny it was to see them push each other towards the career goals they had set. One became resistant and the other would pump energy. To have such best friends is a rare gift from god, who can be selfless and still let you go ahead.

With more chatter, banter and jokes, the day ended. And at the same time, a new journey started. Before retiring to bed, Tiasha had a light dinner. That sounds funny, no? Tiasha and light dinner? Well, it wasn't a choice; the big onions in the vegetables kept her away from food, for the first time perhaps. Having said that, the next day was tougher with half-cooked paranthas, sour curd and a toaster to toast your bread in.

Or perhaps, it was all about perspective because most of the people loved the food. They had always stayed in hostels and PGs and they happily ate the food saying it was better than the food ninety percent of Delhi's hostels served. As for her highness, she had just stepped out of a palace of nurturing and pampering. She just did the task of living there! If it was not her parents, it was Aakaash; if it was not him, it was her favourite Meera didi; and if not her, then Pizza Hut. *Fir ye khana toh agle janam me hi accha lagta!*

Anyway, as Srishti got some food for herself, she asked Tiasha, "Why aren't you having a proper breakfast, Tiasha? It's the most important meal of the day. You must *never* skip it."

She emphasised on 'never' exactly the way her grandmom did.

Tiasha smiled as she looked sleepy. The new place had kept her awake because of the humidity. She desperately missed her air conditioned room.

"My Dadi says the same thing, Srishti. I see her in you. Same generation, aren't you guys from?" Tiasha winked and laughed.

Srishti laughed too. She asked before they entered a five-hour long session on creating good advertisements, "By the way, which is your favourite dish to cook?"

Tiasha became active and energetic all of a sudden. She replied, "Oh, my all time favourite is white sauce pasta. I just love to make it, to eat it and to serve it. And, I believe that's one of the finest dishes I make."

As she narrated her stories of white sauce pasta, they walked towards the class room to study the ethics and rules of advertising. They felt as if college had come back to them.

But,

As Tiasha was mentioning white sauce pasta, it reminded me of something. It was just yesterday that I saw Rakesh in Bikanerwala cooking the same. And it was pretty much close to the situation in which Tiasha was. Just like the olives, capsicum, onions and jalapenos, all the students who were recruited were different but knitted by the cheese of ambition.

When Rakesh added the exact amount of salt and pepper to the brownish vegetables on the induction stove, I saw he added some cheese and kept stirring it for a while. Had I been in his place, I would have just wanted to end the cooking process in five minutes by putting everything in the pan and cooking it around.

But, he waited till the delicious aroma of the pasta attracted almost everyone waiting for it. As he emptied the contents of the pasta into the plate, it looked extremely tempting with the cheese grated over it and oregano sprinkled above the white cheese. Ah! How awesome.

Just like that, when patience and calm stays for a while, ambitions too get knitted with practicalities of life. At the end, producing an extremely delicious and successful white sauce pasta!

Perhaps, it was time to keep that patience for Tiasha. Perhaps.

The steam of a chapati

"Beta, it's 6:30. Get up!"

Tiasha's dad said as he did daily. Every day in Jaipur, he used to wake her up at sharp 6:30 so that she could quickly take a bath in a cleaner washroom. Her highness wasn't used to sharing washrooms, you know. *While I write about Tiasha's tantrums, I just imagine her as a tantrum queen. Do you too?*

Tiasha didn't like waiting, and hostel common washrooms were a good place to test her patience. She rather got up two hours early, took a bath and then slept until her session began at 8:30. Breakfast wasn't anyway worth getting up for, she believed. *Too many issues this girl had, I tell you.*

Tiasha had started getting bored of the life she was living in Jaipur. No roaming out after ten, no going out of the campus – she felt caged.

On the very first day, she argued about boys getting to roam around freely and girls having to stay inside the hostels after ten. What sense did it make, anyway? Just like a trillion hostels with unrealistic curfew times, it was hard for her to believe that Apticon was following the age-old beliefs in the name of 'protocol'. She felt dejected because apart from this stereotype, she found her company pretty cool, and coolness for her was defined by judging them to be non-stereotypical. *Judgemental, yes, she definitely was.*

The case with emotionally vulnerable people is that they pretend to act as if they are strong, but deep inside are breaking each day. And he worst part is, they will never tell you that. Tiasha was one such person.

For the first week, things were new; the second week became dull and since the third started, every day started with a tear of missing home and ended with more tears of missing home. Tiasha had almost stopped having breakfast, lunch or dinner. She just had a packet of chips and lassi in the morning, a few fruits in the afternoon and sweets that they served at night. Adding to that, once, while she was having dinner, she was hungry and in that hunger, she had vegetables, rice and dal. One of those moments when you just feel so hungry that the quality of food doesn't matter. Or perhaps it was her way of pushing herself and accepting things positively.

She sat amidst all her colleagues who were chatting.

"This place is still far better than all the hostels I have been in."

Tiasha's ear became all the more attentive. She wanted to know how these guys were enjoying something which was a big punishment for her. Every day she would kill millions of her wishes for being in the residences – neither could she go back, nor could she cook. She really wanted to know what was the factor that kept everyone else so happy. She all of a sudden felt that the problem was with her and not with the surroundings.

As she thought about this, another colleague added, "True, there's so much beauty around, good food and freedom. I love being here. In fact, I don't want this to end."

'No, no, no. I can't say quiet. I have to question this.' Her mind instructed.

Tiasha questioned, "We are not allowed to move out of our rooms after ten, boys are. What definition of freedom is this?"

"We can anyway slip through, Tiasha. You don't always have to follow rules," a colleague replied wryly.

Tiasha refuted, "I don't think it's about breaking rules. I feel why to have such a rule at all?"

Her colleague replied, "You can't have everything perfectly your way, girl. Ask us who've struggled throughout. We don't get luxury visits to office like you do – we are independent. You'll know when you'll be Can you stop cribbing? If you are bent on finding faults, you will. Can you rather look at the positive side?"

Tiasha wanted to snap back, but she didn't. She just smiled and ended the discussion, "I hope so!"

With that, while ending her meal, she found a bubbly and cheerful fly smiling at her from the vegetable curry. It waved at her with a bright smile. It must have dived into the swimming pool of the curry when Tiasha was busy arguing. Tiasha rejected its smile with arrogance. She got really irritated, kept the plate away and left.

For everyone, Tiasha was a brat who had never struggled and had been over-pampered. You tend to have perceptions about people, don't you?

Everyone thought she was dramatic and hence crying. Some sympathised with her as they felt she was weak. But, no one understood that *different people behaved differently*. If she was breaking in front of the class, it wasn't because she wanted attention, but because she was no longer able to pretend.

Tiasha was the last person who would cry to gain attention. In fact, she was someone who would never show her weakness to the world. Never.

You know, when she came back to her room at 6 p.m., each cell inside her body wanted to give up and tell her to leave. She hadn't eaten well since the last month, she was struggling to get mineral water daily, she hadn't cooked since the last thirty days and a girl like her hadn't seen Aakaash or her family for all these days. No one could see that; they just saw the tests she didn't perform well in. No one was at fault. After all, we judge a book by its cover. Superficial things do force us to make judgements.

When they started, Tiasha was the most intelligent person out of the lot. She did immensely well in advertising her ideas, but as she started draining emotionally, her ideas drained too. Coming to the fifth week, when they had a crucial test on advertising, Tiasha flunked it. She could hardly score 31% and that was enough a reason for people to gossip how she had just acted smart initially but was a dumb head actually. No one bothered to see how every little emotion in her body was breaking her, how the feelings which she felt were her strength, were weakening her. Every day she would think if she had made a mistake coming here, every day while washing clothes in the extreme weather of Rajasthan, she would cry…not because she had to work, but because she was working every minute of the twenty-four hours and yet not feeling content. At times, I feel perceptions make and break us.

Every day, she would ask herself if this is what she wanted from life.

Every day, she would wipe a tear thinking this was just a transition, and things would fall in place.

Every morning, she started her day with a happy smile, sent selfies to Aakaash and her parents, promising herself to be very cheerful.

Every afternoon, she would come back to her room, and pop a pill for headache.

Every evening, she would eat a biscuit or two to push herself for the next few hours.

Every day, she would wash her clothes herself.

Every day, she would wring her heavy jeans and dry them inside her room.

Every morning, she would put up a happy sticky note on the pale wall to make it colourful, and every night, a tear would look at it to confirm that the positivity was slowly evaporating from her body.

Every day, she would talk her to parents, sharing how much she missed home, and every time she spoke to them, she would feel lighter. They would tell her that working was never a necessity, but her choice. As parents, they would never want to see her so miserable and therefore, they told her to come back immediately. But, Tiasha was stubborn. She had decided to take up something and now wanted to at least fulfil it till a year, till the bond ended. Her father told her a lot of times that they could afford giving back the money to her company, but she would refuse saying she would stand by her decision. She did not want to be an escapist.

At the same time, she knew she was the one facing problems and everyone else looked comfortable. She did understand that it was about her crossing her comfort zone. She had to take the challenge and fulfil it, she decided.

Every night, she would hug Aakaash's t-shirt and sleep. She would shift her bed below the fan when she felt suffocated and wouldn't sleep till her eyes refused to stay open. To sleep, she had to have an exhaustive day, else sleep would ditch her, she knew. People slept to relax, her sleep in itself wasn't relaxing.

Every morning, Aakaash would crack jokes to make her laugh. For the first week, she laughed the way she always laughed – contagiously. In fact, she was really happy in the beginning, looking around the lovely nature and the magnificent surroundings. She would walk, talk, and even dance in her room. But, as the days passed, even the best of his jokes failed to make her laugh. Her drowsy face made his life slow, her tears flooded his life with despair and howsoever cliché it may sound, her depression was making him weaker. And those strange feelings were getting weirder. Aakaash did realise that he loved her; he knew he did, just but he wanted to be in denial.

On the one hand, where his solo YouTube video was turning out to be brilliant, her life was taking twists and turns to make her weaker. Ironical, their careers were flourishing, yet they were sad. Aakaash, on the other hand, had kept his video a secret from her. He wanted her to see it as a viral video in three days. He thought it might brighten her face for a moment. To see her bright face, he could easily sacrifice speaking to her and sharing his excitement.

Strange are human desires; never can we ever be satisfied with what we have.

Her life was perhaps more like the steam of a chapati; dangerously hurtful momentarily. But isn't a chapati the only thing which is filling? Exactly like the steam of chapati, these moments make you the strongest.

To get that feeling, you have to go through the steam; you have to fall and you have to get up.

The same night when Tiasha had met the creepy fly in her dal, sleep was evading her. She was the same person, who, fifteen days back, couldn't sleep without having a proper dinner. It was like a foodie being closed in the jails of dieting. *Imagine an Indori deprived of poha jalebi? Yes, exactly that!*

She kept blinking her eyes and kept scrolling the screen of her phone to attract sleep. And staring at the screen of her phone, she slept. At times, it's tough to decide whether the day was meaningful or just spent struggling with ambition. It just becomes too hectic to even realise what you are doing to your life.

And it's exactly then that your heart, mind and body lose track of each other. Being without a purpose makes everything distorted, I believe.

Reiterating, maybe, but Tiasha perhaps was over-reacting, perhaps was dramatic and perhaps was too pampered to stay independently. But, while everyone judged her (somewhere, even I did while writing and even you are while reading), we tend to forget that everyone is different. For someone, breaking rocks is fine, for others it might be tiresome. For someone, being emotional is cliché, for some it might be inevitable. Yes, she was emotional; yes she was protected. But that's okay, isn't it?

Future is as hard to make as khandvi is!

PS: Unexpected, the chapter is.

Tiasha lay on her bed. There was no one in the room but her; there was no energy in her body to get up and switch off the fan as she felt extremely cold. There was no energy in her to search for her medicines. Her body was shivering with fever, each muscle in her body was tearing to make her feel more miserable, her eyes had red arteries visible, and dark brown circles around them, her flawless skin had become darkened, her lips looked dry and brown.

Emotional vulnerability was doing its job, maybe.

She didn't know what to do, she had been lying on the bed like that for the past two hours. She was as miserable as miserable could be.

It was the sixth week of their training and everyone was busy with their projects and deadlines in the conference room even at 2 a.m. Tiasha knew no one was in the hostel. She felt helpless like never before. She felt like she was drowning, and she could sense the feeling of sinking.

Just then, someone knocked on the door. Tiasha felt like an angel had come to her rescue. She somehow managed to open the door and found Srishti with a cup of milk. Srishti couldn't sleep without a glass of milk and just while going back, she thought she'd check on Tiasha. But, as soon as she saw her, she reacted, "What happened?"

Srishti knew Tiasha wasn't coping up too well with the stress of being alone and was taking unnecessary stress just by thinking about it. She told her many times that depression expands if you think you are depressed, but that's the last thing someone with depression could understand.

She touched Tiasha's forehead dramatically, and shouted,

Situations like these are dramatic, aren't they?

"You have seriously high temperature. Wait, I'll get my thermometer and check for the doctor."

She rushed up to her room, got as many things as she could, including a cloth soaked in ice, some biscuits, medicines, thermometer and water. It was adorable to see that timid one carry all these things together. It was her intent, which was pure and honest. She quickly checked the temperature.

The digits were high. It showed 103.5 degrees Celsius.

For a second, Srishti felt nervous, she panicked. But then, gaining a quick sense of responsibility, she dipped the cloth in ice water and placed it on Tiasha's head. Then, she said, "I am going to check for the doctor. You relax, okay?"

Just the fact that someone was around her made Tiasha feel better. She didn't like being alone. Now that Srishti was around, she felt secure. Srishti quickly dialled the trainers and woke them up. After a quick discussion, the trainers concluded, "Taking her to the nearest hospital is the only option, as our doctors aren't available on the weekends."

Srishti replied, "Knowing her condition, she wouldn't be able to walk down. Forget that, she wouldn't even get up."

"What can we do then?" the trainer asked.

"I don't think we have any other option than to wait for the morning," Srishti said.

In the exterior of a city, where the nearest hospital was forty kms away, the doctor was on leave. 'Don't fall sick on weekends, bro!'

Srishti got more ice and some juice for Tiasha. As she came up, she saw Tiasha shivering again. She knew she had to stay with her because medicines would do no good. Still, she gave her a tablet and placed another ice-soaked cloth on her forehead.

Tiasha felt slightly better; at least she had someone around in the most terrible time of her life. Srishti stayed with her... completing her project as well as changing the cloth on Tiasha's forehead. Looked like a mom caring for her little baby.

However, the temperature on Tiasha was as stubborn as her. It stayed at 103 consistently and Tiasha's body wasn't responding to any medication. Perhaps, this was something she had done to herself in the past month as she had not been eating, drinking or taking any nutrients. Perhaps, it wasn't just the illness, but the emotions behind it.

♌

On the other hand, Aakaash was waiting eagerly for the next day. He had uploaded his much-awaited video during the wee hours to get more space on the net and he eagerly waited for the next day to study the analytics of his new gag on the net. He had very high expectations from this video. Tiasha had built those in him, and ironically, she wasn't present when the big day arrived. (Sounds so much like Tiasha had passed away. But, here's me, just adding some drama. You could leniently ignore it!)

In fact, in the past three days, Aakaash was so busy with his marketing team, the production guys and everyone that he didn't even pick her phone once. He wanted to surprise her. Who knew he would be shocked himself! Surprises, ah, surprises!

As he stood with his team to check the increasing views on the projector, they cheered every time a view increased and in less than six hours, they were at 96K views, which by the way was enough for a video to go viral. Everyone cheered for Aakaash as he smiled and thought how his best friend would feel when she'd see the video organically, when it would reach her because of the reach and not by him sending a link. He thought she would feel so proud. And honestly for him, all the views mattered, each comment was special, but the smile he would see on Tiasha's face after his success was priceless. Even more valuable than his success maybe!

And just when the drawing room was full of cheer and beer, Aakaash's phone rang. It was Srishti, who said, "Your best friend is mad. She is refusing to go home because she wants to sit for a stupid test even when she has miserably high fever. I am tired of explaining to her, the trainers are telling her to come back, but because she is a stubborn brat, she won't listen. You just look at her, yaar Aakaash...she really looks depressed. Take her back."

♌

"Tiasha, what the hell is wrong with you?" Aakaash shouted on the phone.

The least he could expect from someone sensible was that they would listen to him when he had travelled 270 kms just in the blink of an eye only for them. However, Tiasha was neither predictable nor sensible. She refused to leave the training mid-way. She wanted to stay till the last week and attempt all the projects and tests.

"Yaar, there will be plenty of tests ahead in office. You can excel in them. For now, for me, just let it go and come down."

Tiasha replied, in a voice less strong, yet firm, "Well, I am not going to escape from any situation, Aakaash. You know that health cannot be a reason to take a break from office ever. I am not weak. I can handle this."

"Who said you are being weak, you idiot? In a condition like yours – you've been having fever for the last two days, had low blood pressure all these days and you are sounding so fucking ill – you and your stubborn nature! Can you please shut the fuck up and walk down with your luggage? These guys will not let me come upstairs, else I would have picked you up and taken you with me!" Aakaash said annoyed.

His voice sounded low and helpless. Normally, Aakaash would be subtle and calm, but when anger struck him, he was an altogether different personality. He was a cloud, peaceful and calm, but once it burst, the rain of anger was passively unstoppable. His silence would tear through the noise and let you know how angry he was.

Although he would never be as rude as he was today, but Tiasha had literally forced him to be so. *Ziddi bachche irritating nahi ho jaate hai kabhi kabhi?* She was being that *ziddi bachcha.*

However, little did it affect her decision. She said, "Who told you to come to Jaipur? Did I call you? No na? Then? You can leave. My decision won't change."

Hearing this, Aakaash was extremely angry. He really wanted to walk up to her room and give his best friend a tight slap. But, he knew that wouldn't work either. In fact, if he became angry, she would never ever in her life listen to him. Gulping all his anger, as he always did, he said calmly, "Listen, your instructors, your office bosses and everyone sane over here feels you should go back home. Do you realise you are creating nuisance for them too by just being idiotically stubborn?"

Tiasha fell quiet. She did know that all her colleagues from office had called her and Naina too had spoken to her. Naina, being the head recruiter, told Tiasha that she could come back and then rejoin when she was fine. In fact, she mentioned, "Tiasha, I know you have been handling too much and that's not your fault. Why are you feeling guilty about it? Just go home and rest. If you feel like coming back, come back. If not, we will have no problem to welcome you directly in the office."

Tiasha, being the most stubborn person anyone would meet, replied, "I agree with what all you say, Naina, but would you feel good if I left mid-way? I don't want to let you down. I don't want to let myself down. I have certain expectations with myself, after all. Anyway, I haven't been performing that well in the tests."

Naina tried explaining to her how much they valued her work, "Tiasha, we've got some brilliant feedback on your work from the first two weeks. In fact, I loved the way you sell the simplest products with a cunning brain. Trust me, these tests are not the basis of judging you. I understand that not doing very well in the tests is troubling you, but that's not because you don't have potential, it's because things are not shaping in an ideal way for you. I believe you should go back and come to office rejuvenated...at least you'll be able to prove yourself there."

Naina tried her best to convince Tiasha, but couldn't. Hence, her only solution was here. Aakaash said, ending the phone call then and there, "Look Tiasha, enough of your nonsense. Every single person on this earth has been telling you to come home and you are behaving like an idiot in an unreasonable manner. I have had enough. No more of your nonsense now. If you don't come down in the next ten minutes, I promise I'll never do comedy again in my life."

Tiasha shouted, as Srishti packed her bags and kept everything inside her suitcase, "Aakaash, stop being..."

Aakaash disconnected the call. Typical of him – when in anger, he would behave in this manner. Tiasha knew he would not step back on what he said. He never did. He wasn't confused like her; he was always crystal clear about things. Even today, she knew if she didn't go back, he would take all his videos down from the net. I told you, he was a cloud, and at this moment, Tiasha knew if she didn't walk down, he would just burst and destroy everything.

She thought for a moment, after which she got up.

Srishti smiled, while packing all the bags. She knew the only force which could convince Tiasha was Aakaash.

Tiasha quietly took off all the stick-on notes which she had stuck on the walls a month-and-a-half back.

She read some of them while taking them off and kept them in a small box. These would, after all, be the memories she would laugh at later on, at how emotionally dependent she was. How she needed small stick-on notes to bring positivity in her life.

'What's the word tired? We decide if we are too weak to get tired.' The first post-it read.

'You are seeing India's best chef in the mirror. Smile at her,' read the neon green post-it which she had stuck on the mirror.

'Smiling helps, tears don't. Stop cribbing because that has helped nobody in life.' The last sticky note on the wall read.

As Tiasha kept all of them inside, she needed to hold on to the table, for her body was weak. Srishti took all her bags downstairs as she told Tiasha, "Get well soon. I really want to learn cooking from you, girl."

Tiasha walked a step ahead and gave her a tight hug. She said, "Never in my life will I forget what you've done for me. Every sprout of yours, every bowl of khichdi that you made and every time you supported me even when I troubled you. I love you yaar."

Srishti gave her a pat on the back and smiling, she took Tiasha downstairs. After three days, she climbed down and saw the world around her. Otherwise, she suffered sleep paralysis, midnight depression and what not! It was like a butterfly had come out of the cocoon.

As soon as she came out and saw Aakaash, she rushed towards him with a drop of tear in her eyes.

She ran and hid herself in his arms. He had tears in his eyes too.

As he looked at Tiasha, tears dropped down his eyes. She wasn't looking fine – her eyes were red, her dark circles were testimony of the sleepless nights, she had almost lost ten kgs of weight in the last one-and-a-half months and her face looked deprived of a genuine smile.

Aakaash cursed himself a thousand times to have kept his ambition and dream above her for the last one month. He knew they hadn't spoken a lot and he knew that if they would have spoken, Tiasha would have fared better. They just spoke for a minute or two because he was too busy. For a second, he wanted to leave everything and just be with her. He felt he was being mean today.

Tiasha, on the other hand, felt extremely secure.

Everyone watched the two of them, some of them recognised Aakaash; they had seen his video. Some felt jealous of Tiasha; she had the cutest stand-up comedian with her, taking care of every little thing. He didn't even let her carry her phone. He handled everything. Her colleagues gave her a tight hug and wished her a warm 'get well soon'.

At that moment, Tiasha felt as if she was amidst family. Yes, there were some people who didn't like her, some she didn't like and that's how life is, but when she needed their wishes, they stood by her. She smiled and waved at everyone.

I know I'm making a very bad comparison again, but just like the midnight eviction in Big Boss, here she was leaving Jaipur mid-way.

♌

Aakaash cleared the back seat of her SUV as he asked her to lie down. Tiasha argued, "I'll sit with you in the front seat and I'll drive half the way."

Aakaash was amused at the drama this girl could do even when she was extremely weak. He simply held her hand and asked her to lie down, covered her with a quilt and kept a little pillow beneath her head as he replied, "No more arguments, Tiasha. Nothing doing."

He removed her bellies and kept them aside as he carefully covered her feet with the quilt.

As he said so, Tiasha could see something which she had never seen before in his eyes. Amidst the dimly-lit SUV, while they were intellectually close to each other, she just held his hands as he was about to push the car's door. Almost pulling him with a jerk, she said, "I feel good. I feel warm now."

Aakaash gave her a smile and said nothing. He started driving towards Delhi when Tiasha looked out of the window. Each light in the dark night appealed to her, each sound of the horn made her feel content and each car that passed re-introduced her to the world outside those residences. She felt so good. She said, looking outside, "I feel free."

Aakaash turned back and smiling broadly at her, he said, "You want to stop and have something Tiasha?"

"Nope. I am not hungry," she replied, wryly.

Perhaps, this was the first time she didn't want to eat. Aakaash tried talking about food and her dishes, but when Tiasha didn't show much interest in them, he immediately felt alarmed.

But, just because he thought that her illness was the reason, he ignored the alarm that his mind signalled. He kept talking to her about random things going on, when he realised that Tiasha had not seen the video yet.

On the other hand, some of her colleagues did walk up to Aakaash acknowledging his talent when he was in Jaipur, but little did it matter to him if she hadn't seen him. She mattered more than the world, after all. He smiled as he drove on to Delhi.

You know, yesterday my Dadi was making khandvi while I was writing. Secretly, I love everything my grandmother cooks. So, on my special demand, when Dadi was struggling to make khandvi with flour and buttermilk, I saw how much patience this dish requires. Dadi calmly kept stirring and cooling the paste until it cooled down completely. Then, she fried it with some leaves and black mustard seeds.

I was pretty much distracted with my grandmother's hard work. And just then, I wondered that making a career is as difficult and requires as much patience.

Much like Tiasha. She was in the testing phase. If she cooled everything properly now, she would definitely end up being like the tasty and successful khandvi.

Zooming out from the picture at the moment, we could see one SUV along the roads of Delhi. Aakaash drove sincerely as Tiasha slept peacefully in the back seat. Once Aakaash did turn to check her and just then he fell in love with her – *once again.*

She slept like a little kid, with the quilt all messed up and the pillow thrown down. Anyone would fall in love with her expression. The dim lights only added to the moment.

As he drove, he thought about them. For the first time did he let himself focus on 'them', instead of each other.

Recovering

It's always in the times when you're most ill that you know who the closest of your friends are.

It was just recently that I fell ill with typhoid, the result of which was a constantly high fever for three days. I didn't know what was happening around in the globe. I just knew my body was shivering with pain and high temperature. On the one hand, when I was perturbed with myself for not being able to eat good food, on the other, I was extremely scared of becoming weaker. There were days when I wasn't even able to stand up. Those were the days when I realised that a few friends can cheer you up at any and every time. Our conference calls never ended as I stay wide-eyed awake throughout the night, even when Chandni and Gautam had a full day at office. Their jokes made my day as I would wait for them to reach home and call me. Hearing all the banter, rubbish and making me hear their banter – what else could make a talkative kid happier? For me, sab kuchh baat karne se sort ho jaata hai!

Such is the power of friendship, I have always believed, just like Tiasha. However, you know what is slightly complicated?

It is when love starts interfering in a happy friendship. When things are going fine, but love starts seeping into the friendship and starts adulterating it with emotions, feelings and complications. Sometimes, it is because of over-thinking and sometimes, it is just sheer destiny. What was brewing here is something I'll leave up to you to decide.

♌

As Tiasha was recovering from her low blood pressure, stomach complications and severe viral fever, Aakaash wouldn't go home and stayed by her side. In the past ten days, he hadn't gone back to his place. He stayed with Tiasha, took her to the doctor, checked her blood pressure ten times a day, made juices, shakes, food, chapatis, and sat beside her when she felt scared. It seemed as if she was the only concern that he had at that point of time.

Tiasha had always loved his company. She did realise that Aakaash was an inseparable part of her life and the love and emotions that grew between them were definitely putting them in a situation similar to mine at the moment.

Sitting at home and munching nachos, I was confused choosing between the salsa sauce and the mayonnaise. Both are tasty, both enhance the taste of the nachos, but at the end, you choose one, right? Friendship and love were the same for them. They either could be best friends for the rest of their lives, like they were, or could take a leap in their relationship.

Ah! Aakaash already had taken that leap in his mind, by the way!

He had not even looked at his Vlog once in those ten days when he was with Tiasha.

His team called him a hundred times a day, but although his phone was on, he was unreachable. Neither did he accept an event's invitation, nor did he attend the success party of his latest video. He just stayed with her day and night. He would get up before Tiasha, would sleep after her, even if she was awake the whole night, which she mostly was. She slept through the day. Then he would oversee the maids and get the house into order and as she stayed up throughout the night, he would stay by her and hear all her nonsense.

It was just one of those nights when Tiasha was in no mood to sleep, she said at ten at night, "Aakaash, let's go and have a pizza."

Viral, throat infection and pizza! Interesting stuff her mind processed. Aakaash, who sat by her bedside, smirked and replied sarcastically, "Yes, let's go."

Tiasha jumped out of her bed at once and while she rushed to change, Aakaash didn't get up from his place. Noticing that, she came back like a little kid coming back to her father and sat on the bed with a sad expression. In a deliberate attempt to butter him, she said, "Please, *chal na.*"

Aakaash was in no mood to be buttered. Anyway, he was extremely stubborn on what he said. He reverted, "I am saying let's go. But, only I'll eat."

"And I'll see your beautiful face, is it?" she snapped angrily.

Aakaash smiled. He reacted rather funny. He said, "They say viral and fever takes over a person's head. I can relate to it when I look at you."

Tiasha got up and started punching him on his shoulder. She then picked up her pillow and thrashed him black and blue. However, Aakaash stayed firm, "We are not going. Or, if you want an outing from home, I'll take you, but not for too long. Okay?"

Tiasha jumped up with excitement again.

"Yayy. Get ready, fast!" she ordered him as she dug inside her cupboard to look for clothes. It was after two months that she had got a chance to go out. First, she had been in Jaipur and then the next consequent ten days, she fell ill. And, for someone who is so fond of eating and tasting junk food, this was truly a tough challenge.

All I can say, after suffering much from typhoid myself is that Tiyu, I relate to you. I was as happy to visit Pizza Hut after two months of eating daal and roti.

ꝺ

As they reached Domino's, Tiasha looked cute in her casual t-shirt, which had Mickey Mouse smiling, and Aakaash looked responsible in his dark brown shirt, which complemented his physique. All of a sudden today, he felt looking after her was something he could do happily ever after.

As they got down at a dimly lit parking, Aakaash said, "Coming to a mall at 10:30 in Noida is no less than going on a rocket mission alone. But, idiots don't understand that."

Tiasha looked at him from the corner of her right eye and made a face. She snapped, "Idiot, you are an idiot!"

Aakaash gave her a teasing expression.

As they got down, Aakaash said, "You better don't order everything and then say, 'I am done Aakaash, *tu kha abb*'. I will not finish your leftovers."

Tiasha said as they entered Dominoes, "Since the last four years, I have been doing that. Habits don't change so easily, baby."

But, the baby hardly heard what she said. He quickly reached the counter and placed the order with her trying to sneak peak. As he paid at the counter and turned, she asked, "What did you order and why was I not the part of placing the order? Such misogyny."

He smiled. That smile of his signified happily that he knew this was coming. He didn't reply until she held him from his elbow and asked, "Aakaash, what have you ordered."

"One onion pizza with less cheese and a Coke."

Tiasha had a disgusted expression on her face as Aakaash casually sat in a comparatively empty outlet. She turned back and went to the counter to place her order as well, but Aakaash's was the last order. She fumed as she walked towards him. She angrily shouted at him as he still had a calm expression while looking at her activities – the to and fro to the counter, I meant! He anyway knew his was the last order for the day.

She shouted, "I don't like onions!"

"That's exactly the reason why I ordered it," he said, calmly, still with the smile on his face.

"You are just intolerable," she fumed.

"I know," he said.

Didn't I mention his eyes still were that tranquil and her eyes were still tumultuous? Similarly, his smile depicted a calm which not everyone's face could handle and her expressions were as dynamic as her nature. She was volatile and he was stable; she was fragile, he was composed, and together, they were an extreme combination!

♌

Anyway, as they sat and spoke about this and that, Aakaash loved to see her laugh loudly. Her laughter was contagious, and his jokes were irresistible. Together, they were a mad combination. Especially today, when they sat in an empty Domino's outlet and chatted happily.

However, the laughter ended soon, when Aakaash snatched the last piece of Tiasha's pizza. She hated sharing pizzas and even though onion, it was a pizza. She had diligently taken out each piece of onion from it, after all. She angrily looked at him and giving him some disgusted expressions, spoke to the glass of Coke on the table.

The poor paper glass.

Tiasha said, "Mr Coke, tell people not to be over-responsible. I can take care of myself."

Aakaash smiled. His smile and her anger were a heady combination, it seemed. He played on, "Mr Coke, why not tell people to shut up and eat."

"What's left to eat, Mr Coke? People are just so mean," she replied.

"Yes, I am a bit mean but I love the person who I am being mean for." Aakaash apparently didn't realise what he said. But, Tiasha did and happily ignored it. She knew it was the flow of his speaking that he hadn't realised. Although for a second, she felt the tickling inside her body too. But, just for a second.

On the other hand, Aakaash felt embarrassed. Although he had said what he really wanted to. He wanted to tell her that he felt happy with her around and without her, he felt lonely. He wanted to tell her that she was his best audience and that she inspired him and that he loved her and that he wanted to tell her that he was totally and madly in love with her. However, he just left the situation mid-way and changed the topic. He loved playing with words, after all.

Emotions were left mid-way, but till when can love leave one alone?

This is one things I trust the feeling called love with. You can try to rush, run and ignore it, but if it has to enter your heart, it will. It certainly will. You can probably choose your priorities right, but feelings are like jugnus. You can't keep them in a box. If you do so, the light will be limited to that box. If you don't, it'll brighten the atmosphere around. So, while you can choose not to give your feelings a name, you can't stay away from them. And, you should not. It's beautiful to feel for someone, it's beautiful to let your heart be at its pace and its beautiful to know that love exists. It certainly is!

Lobongo lotika

Vague emotions are the worst enemy of friendship. They neither let you be *just friends,* nor do they allow you to flow with your feelings. Confusions had perhaps taken the seven vows of marriage with Tiasha. They just didn't want to leave her till eternity.

However, someone else had probably decided to clarify all the confusion in their lives. Yes, three days after he had accidently said what he really wanted to, Aakaash decided to accept what he felt. Being the true blue creative brain that he was, he had figured out the best way to propose to a chef.

Disclaimer: There is some really sweet stuff happening around. You might, like me, feel that '*all this happens only in books*', but let's both not forget that books are the reflection of our minds. And such stories I write because they do exist and I believe in them!

ჲ

As she opened the lid of the sugar box, there was a little note that said,

To 1000 days of friendship.

Tiasha looked at it surprised. She looked at the note with a weird expression, slightly guessing what was going on but still trying to act unaware. She was someone who'd understand everything, yet if she didn't want to acknowledge the fact, she would act innocent.

Aakaash, who peeped in from the outer room, saw her opening the next box for cloves, which read,

10 lakh moments of togetherness

She smiled at this note. Each moment flashed through her mind. The sunsets and their conversations on the terrace, their farewell, their arguments and their tantrums...everything!

She quickly picked up the pan, which had a cute note on it, which said,

Every joke that I say makes me smile only if it can make you laugh. Your laughter rejoices my jokes, your smile rejoices me.

The spoons in her kitchen, which were placed just above the pan in a string had a note on them, which in totality read,

You are the joke I would like to take seriously. Would you want to be the joke that keeps me going?

A stand-up comedian and jokes are inseparable. A stand-up comedian and satire make each other. Comparing her to his joke was no offense, if you felt so. It was the best compliment anyone could give her.

And she felt elated looking at those spoons. She loved it when she thought of them together. *But, together?*

She quickly hid her happiness and acted unaware again. Just as she turned to look at Aakaash, she saw a tiny box and was asked to open it.

As Tiasha opened it, it had a Labongo lotika kept inside it. A Bengali dish, this is made by filling sweet stuffing inside a wheat layer and dipping it in sugar syrup.

Anyway, Tiasha quickly picked the dish up and happily took a bite from it. As she took a bite, there was something hard which hit her teeth. She looked at it to find a beautiful and delicate gold ring.

Now, this was unexpected. This was so beautiful. However, this confused Tiasha the most. She didn't know how to react to gold rings, after all. And the person that she was, confusions would never leave her.

She loved every bit of this special gesture that he did. However, being the typical self that she was, didn't react in an expected manner.

She looked at the ring pensively as she made space for herself to sit on her kitchen's platform. That's where she took all important decisions of her life, by the way. That was her favourite place to think about everything. As she thoughtfully looked at the ring, Aakaash walked inside the kitchen.

"This is the first thing I bought from the money I got from my first viral video, madam."

She didn't reply.

She loved the surprise, yet she was behaving as if she was still thinking. A true blue drama queen this girl was.

And if her reaction was unexpected for us, it was expected for him. He knew her silence. In fact, he made space next to her and sat on the platform, knowing the fact that she would take time to think and sort her confusions. He joked, while sitting, "Thanks to uncle that he made such strong platforms in your kitchen, else these wouldn't be able to carry the weight of both of us."

Tiasha didn't speak a word.

No trace of laughter was visible on her face. All that was visible was the tension that the ring had brought on her face, looking at which, Aakaash said, "*Theek hai yaar. Friend ka gift samajh ke rakh le. Senti na ho.*"

He sat with her for the next ten minutes with no one speaking anything, except Tiasha's brain, but once the atmosphere started becoming sombre, Aakaash jumped off the platform and said calmly, "*Chal*, I'll see you."

He was rather disappointed with her reaction, he was rather angry with the way she behaved and he was much disturbed with his tumultuous feelings. For the first time, he had an ocean of feelings churning inside him. And he definitely couldn't handle them well.

Imagine if a person who eats only boiled food is served spicy and *masaledaar* food. How would he react? *Bas, wahi reaction tha Aakaash ka.*

However, his only visible reaction was leaving the kitchen. No trace of anger reflected on his face, no trace of disappointment reflected in his eyes and no trace of disgrace did he reflect for her. All that he wanted was some time alone. No one can be that understanding to handle a quiet response to a surprise so well planned, after all. Had I been in his place, I would have thrown everything aside and run away.

He thought she needed her space. But, just when he was about to walk away from the platform, Tiasha held him by his elbow and said, "Come back and sit here. I am thinking."

Her expressions were exceptionally cute. He saw one positive ray in the dark kitchen. Just like when you light the stove with the lighter for the first time…that spark was visible to him now.

And as he sat back, next to her on the platform, she said looking away, "I don't like the idea of getting married and all. Too troublesome, these ideas are."

Where did marriage come from, I wonder. You're wondering too?

Tiasha was an extreme over-thinker, man.

Aakaash replied, "So?"

"So? You proposed to me for marriage, didn't you?" she replied, confused.

Aakaash laughed out loud. He said, "*Whaat?*"

He laughed hard. All of a sudden, all his sombre and tumultuous expressions changed into sarcastic ones. He looked extremely hot with his smirk and spark in his eyes.

She looked so cute with such apologetic expressions, he thought as he looked at her.

Tiasha looked at him with confused expressions. Gifting a ring with an 'I love you note' meant that, didn't it? Her eyes asked him a thousand questions. He, while laughing, said, "You think I want you to marry me? Idiot."

He, while laughing, wrapped his arms around Tiasha's neck and said, "I don't want to get arrested for marrying a kid. I just wanted to tell you...that..."

"That?" Tiasha looked at him from the corner of her left eye and asked super innocently.

Aakaash didn't say anything. Tiasha asked again, "*Bata na* Aakaash. That?"

Now, she was the authoritative buddy to him.

He smiled and said, "That, I love you. I find inspiration in you."

Tiasha smiled. Her cheeks were red now. He should have said this earlier; he would have got an instant answer. The tension of marriage made her so pensive. She was a kid, he reiterated to himself as he smiled looking at her. Keeping her head on his shoulder, she said, "You scared the hell out of me. As far as love is considered, I love you too!"

She smiled broadly. After a pause, she continued, "But choosing me is your choice, and you always have a choice, as you say! I'll be this brat...don't expect me to change."

Aakaash looked straight into her eyes and replied in the most assuring tone that he could, "Anything but this would ever happen."

Tiasha smiled broadly, knowing very well that what he said was absolutely true!

And zooming out from here, the kitchen looked like the sweetest part of the house. With the sugar boxes, cloves and pans smiling at the love that just blossomed, the two of them sat on the platform of the kitchen with laughter surrounding them. For a second, I just want to freeze this moment. Everything looked perfect. Didn't it?

And, just like Lobongo lotika, the sweet-filled feelings which were stuffed inside the outer layering of the heart finally came up to the lips. Expressions finally got visibility in the tough argument between the heart and the mind.

Part - III

Captain!

'Bhaiya, corporate mein toh bosses se do hazaar kilometre door hi rehna.'
'Bosses torture karne ke alawa kabhi kuch bhala kar sakte hain?'

Thanks to all the Bollywood flicks and television operas, our brain has stereotyped the word 'boss' as someone torturous, mean, cunning and finicky. The moment someone says boss, we laugh out loud at the jokes, or perhaps sympathise with our friend while listening to his 'boss-tales'.

On the day Tiasha joined work in the office, the first thing she wondered was, 'Who will be my boss? How will he/ she be? What will the day be like?'

One, she was joining all her colleagues almost after a month. Two, she was, as always, apprehensive at the start. Three, she had a bubble of excitement in her mind which was making her too lively, just opposite to how everyone had seen her always.

I believe the moment we add the word 'first', there's a new feeling inside our hearts. The first crush that we had, the first date we went on, the first rains with your loved ones, the first day of school, the first day in college and, of course, the first day at work. Every new journey brings with it waves of positive energy and opportunities. It is all up to us how we grab them. Either we could make the best out of the first or perhaps struggle in the journey – it all comes from within.

♌

Just if you forgot, Tiasha had to join office with her colleagues, who had attended the full training at Jaipur. She resumed her work in Gurgaon directly and this was her first day at office.

Luckily, for Tiasha, this beginning was devoid of any confusion. She was happy to stand in front of the building of her new office – Apticon Solutions. As she filled her details in the visitor's register, she excitedly spoke to the guard, "*Aur bhaiya. Abb toh aana jaana laga rahega yahan.*"

The guard smiled. Tiasha walked inside to the reception, where Naina, along with the team leads was waiting for the new employees of Apticon. Looking at Tiasha, she got up and gave her a tight hug. She said, "I am very happy to see you. How are you?"

Tiasha smiled broadly and replied, "At the moment, very excited. The office looks so pretty, Naina."

Naina smiled. Every year when the campus students joined office, they had the same glitter in their eyes; they were almost jumping into a transition from campus to corporate. Naina, being very observant, always saw this charm in the eyes of those who joined the office.

She asked, as they moved inside and Tiasha greeted the other team leads as well, "So, got all your tests done? How is your health now?"

"Yes, the reports were all normal…just some haemoglobin and blood pressure complications. Trivial ones. I'll be fine," Tiasha replied, positively.

Naina joked, "I am glad to see how easily you make these complications sound so trivial."

They shared a short laugh after which they entered the conference room and introducing Tiasha to her project lead, Naina said, "Mohit, you have a chef in your team, it seems."

Tiasha smiled looking at Mohit, who was dressed professionally in business formals. He looked extremely well dressed in his official formals and had a pair of observant eyes. Tiasha took note of that immediately. And immediately made an image comparison in her head.

Looking at herself in the mirror of her conscious, she created a quick imagery with her wearing a casual t-shirt and jeans on her first day to office. Pretty decent versus pretty casual was the exact inference that her mind delivered.

Mohit formally smiled. He, for once judged her by her clothes – wavy hair left open, a casual t-shirt with donuts printed on it and a pair of baggy jeans.

'Lovely!' he sighed to himself. 'Kids,' he sighed again.

It happens, when you yourself are very conscious about your clothes, it becomes obvious that you like well-dressed people as well. An example of that is your author too. I have an obsessive compulsive disorder about the creases on my clothes. That is, that I don't wear clothes till every single crease is gone. And this is not today but since school time that I don't compromise on clothes and that's apparently the reason I appreciate well dressed people a lot. On the contrary, when I see my friends having their sleeves rolled up shabbily, I make sure to correct it.

Anyway, Tiasha just felt happy to be in Mohit's team. I wish the feelings were mutual.

However, to Naina and the others, he replied, "Oh! That's great. We'll have good food every day at lunch then."

A true blue corporate lead, he was. He knew to handle his expressions and opinions very well. In fact, I have learnt something working for almost a year now – if you have a good manager, it's not that you get everything perfect, but at least, you get a way and motivation to handle everything, even escalations.

Recently, I was annoyed about something at work. What helped me was not sulking or cribbing, which I had almost become used to, but to reach out to my manager. 'Heart is for home, leave it when you decide to step inside the office,' he said when I shared my list of concerns. Perhaps that was something my brain quickly registered. It made so much sense to solve problems. For a moment, I didn't feel there were problems, even when there were many.

'You are going to get stinker emails from me going forward, but that's how I work. Your work should be to overcome that. Don't repeat it and then that solves a lot of problems. Escaping them won't.' That was the response. It actually helped me get a perspective. Being emotional is good, but these office experiences have taught me a lot. Though I've just had a few of them!

Let's anyhow come back to Tiasha.

Tiasha smiled formally.

'Thankfully, at least the smile is formal. I was expecting a high five from this one,' Mohit said to himself. At the same time, he remembered his first day in office when he came dressed in a t-shirt and jeans. Life takes a full circle and brings you back to the same point, he thought nostalgically.

Just like the corporate culture, it takes time and a journey of experience to change from casual to formal, after all.

Tiasha, on the other hand wondered, 'He looks decent but is too formal. Maybe fifteen-twenty years of experience does that to you!'

As they chatted and judged each other for a while, Naina broke the silence and said, "Tiasha, you would be working for Choko Majista, which is by the way one of the leading clients that we have. We've helped them grow in India by providing them with the best ads that they could get. Mohit has been leading the project since we got it in 2012. It is a flourishing account. Plus, it's food. I am sure you'll do good."

Tiasha replied, "Definitely Naina. I will."

Mohit took over, saying, "Good. I like the zeal."

Tiasha was the only recruit who was assigned to Mohit's team. Being the team lead, he got up as soon as Tiasha was introduced and said, "Come, let's go. I'll take you to our team."

Naina signalled a best of luck through her eyes to Tiasha as she continued introducing the rest of the recruits to their respective bosses. As Tiasha walked up to the third floor of the gigantic corporate office that she was now part of, Mohit said, "Liking the work place, Tiasha?"

"Yes Mohit. It's wonderful. In fact, this is so much better than Jaipur."

He laughed as they climbed the stairs. Mohit mentioned proudly that he never took the elevator while they climbed up the third floor. Tiasha was left with no option but to accompany him, huffing and puffing, silently though!

He said, "You came back from Jaipur sooner, didn't you?"

While huffing and stealing breaths, she replied, "Yes. I couldn't keep pace with the food, schedules and atmosphere there."

'Too honest and innocent for the corporate world!' he spoke to himself. To her, he replied, "Oh. You'll have more of all these here. And I don't approve leave too easily. I hope you won't need to leave this mid-way too."

Tiasha replied in a slightly blunt tone, "I don't think I leave things mid-way till there's a situation I am not able to handle. I didn't want to leave the training mid-way; I was almost thrown back to Delhi to recover." She tried to keep a smile on her face as she said so.

Typical of me, I would say. Whenever I feel bad, it reflects too easily on my face. I'd hardly speak a word, but I know my expressions speak a lot. And, I have been trying to solve this for a year now, but habits are habits. And bad habits are even harder to shake off.

'Aggressive too,' he noted to himself. To her, he said as he opened the gate for her, "That's okay. You guys still are kids. It will take time. Anyway, come let's meet the team. I'll introduce you to your supervisor."

As they walked towards the cubicles where the employees were busy resolving issues and finding statistics, Mohit announced loudly, "Guys, we have Tiasha here. Let's quickly welcome her. See you in the meeting room in five."

Saying so, he escorted Tiasha. He was experienced and sharp, but at the same time, he knew it was her first day. Switching off his judgemental stance as he sat inside the meeting room, he said in a warm tone, "See Tiasha, it will take some time to adjust, as the team we are a part of is gigantic. We work with the media and animators almost as closely as punctuation would be with a word. And everybody has a unique way of working. Initially, they would not want to take you seriously. They'll throw away your creative ideas because changes are difficult to implement and it takes more effort. But, just remember one thing – you are a creative advertiser. Creativity in content should be your forte; don't let anyone pressurise you and don't panic about being unheard. This will happen, but sail through. I assure you, if your idea is good, I'll make sure you get all the resources to implement it!"

He smiled at her. Tiasha, who by now was judging him to be judgmental, brushed away those thoughts at once and smiled broadly at him. She saw a mentor in him that very moment.

In the meantime, the team quickly gathered in the meeting room.

Mohit said, "So, we have a new team member. She's Tiasha Shah and will be working as a creative advertiser in the content team. Anushi, you'll supervise her work for the first two months."

Anushi looked at him and then at Tiasha and smiled. She replied, "Sure. That'll be great."

As Tiasha looked at her new supervisor, she saw a simple yet firm face in Anushi. Wearing a white and blue shirt, her supervisor looked sophisticated and decent to her in the first impression.

After the other twenty-five team members left as soon as the formal introduction was over, Mohit told Anushi, "Make a thirty-day training plan and start giving mocks to her from today itself. I am sure Tiasha is in safe hands. Make sure you prepare her for conflicts and problems as well."

Anushi nodded and smiled.

ᔕ

Walking towards her cubicle, Anushi told Tiasha, "I believe if you have your workstation next to me, it would be good. Will you be fine with that, Tiasha?"

Tiasha thought for a second. As per the rule that Bollywood taught her, she should have said no. She should have stayed away from her boss. However, breaking that rule in her mind in that millisecond, she replied, "Of course. That would be absolutely fine, Anushi." Both of them smiled at each other.

There were positive feelings immediately floating between them.

Placing her bag on the desk, Tiasha felt comfortable sitting at her workstation. The cubicles were spacious and comfortable. The feeling was even more spacious. To have one's own room, to have one's own space in itself is a matter of comfort, isn't it?

While they sat, Anushi noticed the seriousness and some anxiety on Tiasha's face. Being in the company for three years and having survived the corporate culture for the previous five years, she did understand that the atmosphere at times could be overwhelming. However, she knew preaching anything at that moment wouldn't help. She just observed and kept it to herself.

♌

For the next few days, each day was tiring. With tons of mocks and brainstorming sessions that Tiasha was attending, her advertising skills were improving for sure. Every day she would know how a simple chocolate could be sold in hundreds of ways. And just then, when she learnt so much, she would regret being confused for the longest time in her life on taking up this job.

Tiasha gelled well with her team members, but spoke less. She was sweet to everyone but limited her conversations. The other side of the same person was her workaholic and panic-stricken mode. She would stay till wee hours to complete the assigned tasks and finish them before the next day; she would work even after reaching home and would just target the completion of her tasks. Stubborn – yes, she was.

Mohit was extremely impressed by her zeal to work and so was Anushi as a supervisor. But, as a mentor, she felt she needed to spend more time with Tiasha to explain how *work worked.*

Following the same, the next morning when Tiasha exchanged a cheerful good morning with her, Anushi asked, "You've had breakfast?"

Tiasha replied, "No, didn't get the time to go down."

Anushi replied, "I have no company today. Will you come with me?"

Tiasha respected her immensely. Plus, being Tiasha, she would never let anyone have a meal alone. She agreed and while they ate the delicious chowmien that Anushi had made, Tiasha said, "Trust me, you make the best chowmien. Even better than I do. And that day...you remember you had brought chowmien?"

Anushi looked puzzled. Tiasha continued, "Arey, that day when you offered it to all of us? A week back maybe. I had really liked it, but I was too hesitant, and didn't have more of it. Secretly,

I admire your cooking skills since then. And the truth is that I love Chinese food."

Anushi laughed at her innocence. Now she knew why Tiasha became so serious and quiet at times; she just needed a comfortable space to open up, and then she was a chatterbox.

Anushi said, "I'll get more for you, now that I know you like it so much. But, I had something that I had to discuss with you, Tiasha."

Tiasha's expression suddenly changed to sombre. The last few days had probably made her a nerd at office. Anushi observed her expressions and said, "Arey baba, relax. Just generally..."

Tiasha sheepishly smiled and focussed on her noodles, which waited for her, entangled in the fork.

Anushi continued, "See Tiasha, being your supervisor I would be the happiest person if you work day in and day out. I would absolutely have no problems with it. But, having some experience, I would suggest, let go of things at times. You are too serious about work, which is very good. But, you are neglecting your own priorities.

"I am not saying work less, but work with a calm mind. Being panicky will never help. Keep yourself cool while you work. And try managing stress. And if there's anything else, you know you can walk up to me anytime you want."

Tiasha carefully heard Anushi speak, after which, she said in her happy way, "Aye aye Captain!"

At times, we tend to get finicky about small things, trouble ourselves with unnecessary stress, but whether it is needed is a question worth asking yourself. It hardly takes a minute to panic and harm your mental peace, but whether the panic is worth it or not is something you would have to decide.

You know this happens. A few months ago, I felt I knew nothing in my workplace. This probably would sound like a teleshopping ad, but can't help it, this story is relatable. Bear with me. I am sure you can!

So, when I started working, I felt I was clueless. Every time I made a mistake, I would learn not to repeat it, and then, I made a new mistake. The accumulation of this was the team connect, where your author cried. Rare is a moment where a normal team connect with your manager ends up becoming a melodramatic motion picture. With me, I started with a tear in my eyes and hilarious, as that may sound now, I cried like a little kid.

Till date, I do remember the look on my manager's face, asking me what had gone so wrong that I was this upset? Of course, any sane person would feel awkward with me crying for no good reason. He tried telling me I was doing well, but me being me, did not stop until I realised a few days back that cribbing or crying never helps. I was stubborn in emphasising that I didn't know anything too. I am happy to acknowledge that I was wrong. I was simply, as my Metro buddy says, over-thinking. Zyada dimaag hai na, kharch toh karna padega kahin na kahin!

Yes, we build up situations in our head, panic for no good reason, and get perturbed about the smallest issues possible. But there's still something good about it; you grow as you move on. And overcoming the fear of going wrong is the biggest. *Naya naya kuch bhi karo toh problem toh hoti hai, but* I am sure, *uss problem ka solution bhi hota hai.* Focus on finding that solution because if you get that, things will eventually fall into place.

Anushi was trying to explain this to the kid that she was dealing with. At times, she did feel that she had a kid in her team, who could be as chirpy as ever and as tearful as ever, all at the same time. Extreme, Tiasha was!

Some conversations tend to bring a new perspective to your life. Many times, I emphasise that conversations help find out solutions which you probably would not have figured out yourself. Some people, probably are that sorted that when you talk to them, life starts looking like a sorted notepad. Perhaps, Anushi was one such person for Tiasha, who made life look easier and office look happier.

Tiasha, once and for all, had a captain in office who she knew that she could walk up to for anything and everything.

And, trust me, having that one person in the office to whom you could crib about everything – from the travel time to badly cooked dishes – is important. *And just when I preach so much, I realise this looks like a self help on 'How to go to Office'.*

Pyar wyar ka chakkar hi complicated hota hai

The transition from friendship to love isn't a very celebrated one, I believe. While there are many movies that valorise the transition from friendship to love, at times, love can complicate things further.

Almost after a month of the wonderful ring shining on Tiasha's petite finger, things were pretty lovely and mesmerising. Everything was the same like it was earlier – Tiasha and Aakaash spent as much time as they did earlier, they fought like kids, went for dinners together, made instant long drive plans – everything remained as great as earlier.

You thought I'd say so?

Well...

Not really! There was a new guest in between the two of them. It was called expectation!

With a round of applause, welcome expectations, my friends. The gentleman who is apparently the root cause of frustration, the root of any turbulence, the epicentre of the chaotic earthquake of feelings and ego – Mr Expectation.

I have always believed that best friends can end up being good partners; there's a lot of scope for them to be together. However, the only condition is that the expectations they have from each other should be absolutely zero, because friendship apparently is devoid of all expectations and tantrums.

Moving ahead with time

Both of them were an adorable couple as it is, even when they were just best friends, they had almost been like a committed couple. They shared sweet greetings through messages, stayed in each other's vicinity the whole day and would not get tired of each other's company even in their wildest of dreams.

Aakaash was still the same, perhaps he was even more caring towards her. Actually, to be precise, it perhaps wasn't about care. He had actually reprioritized his life over Tiasha. Remember the Aakaash who refused the interview with such confidence to achieve his dreams? Anyone looking at him would have envied his zeal to achieve their dreams. Many a times, Tiasha took inspiration from his stubborn motivation, which was inspirational, indeed!

Ironically, he had kept her above those qualities and dreams. For him, she was his only priority and for her, he was sliding down the list of priorities. She had just entered a new regime and was trying very hard to survive there. In between all this, how was she supposed to find time for herself?

In fact, their love story, which had just started a few days ago, was going in two equally opposite directions. I remember standing at the Rajiv Chowk Metro station and waiting for the Metro. While

I stood there, there would be two Metros crossing each other, going in two opposite directions. Tiasha and Aakaash too were moving in equally opposite directions. If he had started making her his priority, she had started assuming that when no one else understood her at the workplace, at least she could expect his support, which she assumed was always there. And I would say, support actually was always there; just the perception of looking at that support changed. *You know how we can just not indulge in problems? Simply by thinking less. Else, you'll end up complicating everything around.*

At this time, when she had a corporate 9-5 job, an impending cooking competition, which could change the dimensions of her cooking career, and many ambitions floating evidently in her life, perhaps a relationship was the last thing she would want to get into.

In between work, there was no time that she could spare for love.

Every day, she would get up at six, travel to Gurgaon in the Metro, or on some rare occasions, in her car, she would work till five, reach home by eight and then prepare recipes for herself till eleven. With such a schedule, she had no energy left to meet or greet anyone. One thing is that you don't have time and the other is you don't have the zeal. With her, both of them stood true.

Plus, her relationship was more like a routine for her now, and if love becomes a routine, how do you expect one to be cheerful? We are never excited about routines, right?

It was anyway a pretty bad time to complicate things. These two had chosen to jump into the well, it seemed, when all Tiasha had on her mind was work and food. She wanted to test her capabilities in the office, and wanted to prove her mettle in her passion too. Lucky are those who get both, I must say!

Many times, we are in a zone where all we see is an aim. A goal.

Chandni and Gautam, my virtually permanent room-mates, once declared while we were discussing about relationships and life

– once in a lifetime do we get into a conversation as serious as this one with the closest of friends. While discussing the permutations and combinations of love and relationships, they ended up making one marked observation.

"It's good to be in love until you have a dream as stubborn as yours."

I agree as well. With the kind of madness that I have for my work, I myself fail to reassure myself that I could fall to the gravitational force of love. There are moments in your life you would never want anything to distract you away from what you love. Not even someone you have adored and admired.

Tracing my journey, it isn't that I was an alien who dropped in from Mars and had no feelings for anyone ever. It's just that I preferred walking away from that space of love and feelings because there was one thing which my life had decided to take seriously since I was sixteen. And that's perhaps the reason I never fell in love! And that's why, it's easier for me to relate to Tiasha's situation. I don't know if you can too.

Some dreams are mighty and they need sacrifices. Some genuine feelings are difficult to be sacrificed, but at times, to build an empire of dreams, you have to let go of something, be it feelings then! Just that saying so is far easier than doing it. When the feelings are true, perhaps it wouldn't be as easy to make a choice then. Ah!

♌

It was a busy weekend for Tiasha. She was busy working on one of her recipes and was jotting it down. Aakaash, slightly disappointed with the plan ahead sat next to her and was scrolling through the comments on one of his previous videos.

This tends to happen. When you start sticking on to the past, how do you make a new future? The book that you are reading too passed through that phase. Perhaps, too much of information but if readers are family, they should be knowing what's happening with their family member, shouldn't they?

So, yes, while I wanted to juggle between writing and work, I was unable to do so. I am perhaps the kind of person who wouldn't ever learn if I am humiliated or pin-pointed. I'd rather learn only with a humble approach. And that was, perhaps is, one of the biggest weaknesses that I have. One nasty comment at the workplace and I would end up thinking about it for the whole day for no good reason. I must have wasted some thousands minutes thinking about things which were to be ignored!

But, it happens. There are phases. Rough ones are trickier. They work only when you let yourself work harder.

That was the rough patch in my journey – where I was lingering on the memories of *No Matter What I Do* to be satisfied. An earlier version of the same author would have rather created new memories to reach ahead than staying with the older memories – good or bad. Anyway, as Papa tells me, "Think effectively, but think less. Over-thinking will do no good."

Staying with my grandparents here in Delhi, they've actually seen the worst of me – doing absolutely nothing and just thinking that 'I am not able to write'. It is already difficult to handle a chatterbox workaholic at home. Over and above that, they were handling a disturbed chatterbox workaholic now. But, it's just their belief in my work that I bounced back after trillions of calls to my parents, a hundred conversations with my grandparents and the Metro journeys!

That reminds me of the one of the conversations with my Metro-buddy. While we were returning home, we were discussing work and stress (I laugh while saying stress), when while discussing he finally concluded, 'Take things seriously, but don't take everything seriously. Some things are to be peacefully ignored.'

It is only when I realised this that I started to move on with future. That is how your author came back on track. Trust me, from my experience, looking back at the past doesn't help; looking ahead and making a new future does. This was a phase of my life which taught me the most and affected me the most as well, and therefore, I felt there was the need for me to share this with you.

Metro journeys have always been special for your author. I ended up completing this book in the Metro, after all!

P.S.: Just when you thought we were having a motivational lecture, let's move on to Aakaash's life. He was doing the mistake that I learnt from – he was sticking to the past when creating a new future was an option. Plus, he was also making the one mistake, that I never would have – prioritizing his love over the dream that he had woven for himself!

Expectations

While Tiasha took a break from her office work and checked her email that weekend, she exclaimed, "Oh my god!"

Aakaash, who was still browsing through his videos looked up and gave her a questioning look. His expression lacked the charm that a buddy had for Tiasha.

Ignoring his disinterested expression, Tiasha walked up to him and said authoritatively, "Your best friend here is so happy and you—"

Tiasha had a habit of being extremely excited about small things, which at times was slightly immature, but if she had always been taken care of by Aakaash, why would she care?

She was like the weather of Delhi; she liked behaving in extremes. Either she was extremely elated like the showers of rain that poured over Delhi and brought life to the monotonous environment, or she could be like the extremely cold winters of Delhi, which were so chilly that they could curb any emotion from flourishing. Luckily, she was in the former season today.

Extremely happy, excited and elated, she didn't even observe Aakaash's expression. It was always a given for her that Aakaash would be joyful if she was happy. He never behaved the other way round, after all. She knew her happiness meant his smile!

She was really busy being happy and cheerful that she had no time to think about anything else. Her eyes had a spark and her smile looked delightful. Every time she was smiling, she was blossoming like a newly-born petal. This had to be something about her cooking! There had to be something special.

However, when Aakaash didn't look up and still kept scrolling on his screen, Tiasha snatched his phone, saying, "And look at you! Busy with your phone."

"Give me my phone," Aakaash said coldly. His voice was patient but his feelings were not.

Have you ever noticed that when you keep milk over the stove and forget to switch the stove off, the milk, which was boiling pours out of that pan. I tend to always forget when my nani tells me to switch if off, and later on, I end up cleaning the whole stove.

Aakaash's feelings were exactly like the milk, which was on the verge of spilling and Tiasha behaved pretty much like me – ignorant of the situation.

Aakaash told her once again, sipping in all the anger that was accumulating inside him, as he did normally.

"Tiasha, don't behave like a kid. Give me my phone."

If he was calm, she was a bubble of excitement. And at that moment, she looked extremely joyous. She didn't pay attention to him and kept teasing him, playing with his phone.Tiasha did not realise that he was serious, which ended up making Aakaash shout, "Don't you understand? I need my phone!"

Pin drop silence.

No one spoke, no one exchanged a single glance. Only Tiasha's eyes spoke odes about her heart. She felt like the onion which she had removed from the delicious pizza – ignored and alienated. She wanted to give him a tight slap, but she didn't; she just turned and rushed into her room and sat on the floor, with her arms folded around her pillow and tears streaming down from her eyes.

Just as the tears showed up, Aakaash felt guilty. Was he the same person who had re-prioritized everything in his life to keep her on the top of his priority list? He wondered. She was so elated just about a few minutes back. He broke into a smile when he looked at the table and saw the mail from the World Food Festival. The mail said that Tiasha had been appreciated by one of the best chefs for her recipe in their newsletter. Even before they started with the month-long food festival, Tiasha's recipes were creating a buzz among the chef circuit. The best part about that mail was that James, editorial head of the organising magazine, *Cakes and Cuddles* had appreciated her recipes calling them, 'innovative engineering of food'.

No wonder she was that happy, he thought. Then he turned towards the room where she was. She had never been talked to the way he had spoken to her. She had never been told to shut up. Nobody shouted at her. Then, when the closest person behaved in such a manner, how could she take it?

He knew that in her excitement, she had happily ignored his anger and it was justified as well! And, it wasn't the first time she had snatched his phone. But perhaps it was the first time he had snatched away that mesmerizing smile from her face, rather than multiplying it two-fold.

He took a step towards her when he took a turn and left for his place. He knew talking to her now wouldn't make any difference. He knew, she wouldn't hear him out and he knew he was wrong. Rather, he took a back step and walked back towards his place – a world he didn't like being in.

ꝺ

Lying down on his bed, staring incessantly at the ceiling, Aakaash wondered what had happened to him. I remember describing him as a tranquil shelter, which could give shelter to a hundred wandering souls. Today, he was that wandering soul himself. He was introspecting on what was going wrong since the day they had got into a relationship – perhaps, he missed plenty of opportunities just for the sake of being with her, perhaps he missed a lot of events just to make an evening eventful by going on a dinner date with her.

Careers are not built on dates, he reiterated to himself as he still tried to figure out the reasons for why he was behaving the way he was.

He immediately got up when his parent's comments echoed in his ears. He did not want to prove them right by ignoring his career; he did not want to prove himself wrong by not making a mark in the comedy circles; and he did not want to prove the idea of a 'decent' job correct by failing in his own expectations.

He rather wanted to see the Aakaash who had casually rejected a ten lakh job to achieve his dreams; he rather wanted to be the Aakaash who loved his best friend, but cared about her career more than he cared about her. He wanted to be the best friend that Tiasha had.

While walking inside his bedroom, thinking about how the previous days had changed her as a friend, Aakaash realised that perhaps love was not meant for both of them. Tiasha liked spending time outside rather than with him. She liked staying back late in office to work than to have dinner with him. These were the minute changes which were taking a toll on his life and the reason was simple as keeping expectations from her.

Just that very moment, he saw a butterfly flying freely outside his window. Tiasha was that butterfly, who couldn't be captured in a box or kept inside the house; she wanted to roam around freely.

She needed her space and realising that, Aakaash walked into her house, not as a boyfriend who wanted his girl to stay with him but as a *chuddy buddy,* who wanted to celebrate her success with her.

♌

Tiasha, on the other hand, tightly hugged her pillow and sobbed.

Of course, no one ever spoke to her in such a tone. But, for a change, ego wasn't the hassle here; it was the change that she was observing in Aakaash. Not that she did not have any expectations from their relationship, but his were unrealistic, she believed. She wasn't crying because Aakaash shouted at her – that was still fine – they both shouted at each other when they fought. But, each tear in her eyes was because she was missing her best friend all these days.

You know, some people are meant to be left free. They might love spending time with you, but the moment you ask them to spend time with you, you become a burden. And it's always preferable to be the person whom someone would love to talk to, than being a burden. Tiasha was someone from that category.

She loved it when he made her feel special on dates and dinners, but she hated it when on all those dates and dinners, all she wanted was her best friend to accompany her. Office was anyhow tiresome and when a person comes back home, they expect a friendly hug, rather than all the conversations about their relationship and love. Perhaps, it was becoming over-burdening for her. That too when there were too many twists and turns going on in her career. At this point, she missed her best friend miserably.

Strangely, both of them were still on the same page, but of different novels, it seemed!

Rebonding

Just a few days back, while I was having a hair cut and talking to my hair dresser, I realised there is a process called rebonding, where they take some chemicals and give nutrients to the hair. While he was talking about bonding hair, I just wondered if we could make life as simple as a hair cut?

As my stylist gave me a good trim, he brushed away all the split ends. Wish we could remove all the burdensome expectations as easily and replace it with a new style in our relationships. Like rebonding rebonds the hair, why can't we rebond relationships with the chemical commonly called 'understanding'?

Aakaash, being somehow more sensitive, walked towards Tiasha's house and entered her room.

He knew she would not even want to see his face. He knew she was extremely angry and he knew he could be easily slapped in that moment, but he still walked and sat next to the bed where she was crying. He didn't say much, just put his arms around her and gave her a tight hug.

Tiasha didn't even look at him but Aakaash didn't leave her for a second. He said, "I know I am an idiot. I also know that I don't know how to please people and I know I am an idiotic box of garbage. But I am your best friend. *Chal, jaldi se* it's okay *bol de.*"

Tiasha sobbed.

Hearing her sobbing, he felt bad but in a way, he felt good – at least this argument made him realise the importance her career had for him and his dreams got energised looking at her excitement. He knew where he wanted to go. Therefore, the guilt was replaced by ambition, positive one, of course.

Aakaash just said, "Tiasha, I will not go on the stage if—"

Tiasha got up at once and landed her palm of his cheeks. Giving him a tight slap, she immediately hugged him. After a very long time, she felt as if she had got her best friend back, whom she could hit, punch, shout at and trouble. She wrapped herself around him and felt like not leaving him for even a minute. She said,

"You idiot...not every time will I give in to this blackmail."

Aakaash smiled, embracing her, and said, "Not every time do I use it. It's my secret weapon, you see. It's used effectively in situations that need it."

She hit him on his back as they rejoiced the rebonding and cajoled over their friendship. Joy was evident on both their faces. At least, the argument gifted Tiasha her best friend and Aakaash, his career.

Doesn't it happen to you? At times, there are some dreams which need sacrifices, and some that need you to sacrifice your feelings, because feelings can complicate things. I'm not saying that if you have to achieve something, stop falling in love or feeling the feeling called love, but if there's one goal that you have in life, you have to let go of the smaller happiness that these feelings give you. Of course, we are, as humans, vulnerable to feelings, for love can happen anywhere and with anyone. You can't add a filter to your brain when you fall for someone...you just do. For me, I don't normally talk a lot about feelings and love in my personal life, but if I had to describe love in a word, I would probably end up calling it 'respect'. As funny as it may sound, my definition of a date is just having an extremely meaningful conversation with my partner about my as well as his work.

Maybe that's how workaholics think! Also, it's not that my heart is made up of some cells which ceases it to feel or get attracted towards someone. It definitely does. But, every time I look at my dreams ahead, I realise these feelings, howsoever beautiful, I can let go of. For anything else but my love for my dream, I know I have slowly let those feelings go which were always unsaid and unheard of.

Secretly, those unheard and unsaid feelings are perhaps the most truthful ones. We never express them and therefore, they are never adulterated with any expectations!

ର

"So, what's the plan ahead?" Aakaash asked, sitting next to Tiasha while she drove.

"What plan?" she quipped, as she drove along the empty highways of Delhi.

These friends were real jokers. One second they fought, the other second they were back to being the closest confidants. Just like today, they had had a bitter conversation in the morning but just like the hot chocolate sauce over white vanilla ice cream, their anger had melted over the brownie of their friendship and here they were – along the lost roads to find themselves. As Tiasha drove towards India Gate, her favourite late night destination in her favourite city, she looked relaxed.

It was almost after three weeks that she had taken this break. She desperately needed it, trust me. Looking at her dark-circled eyes, anyone could guess that easily!

Aakaash asked, looking towards her with his hazel-eyed gaze, "I meant, what are you planning for the food festival?"

For a second, Tiasha felt that his concern was fake. How come someone who had ignored her conversation in the morning was being so concerned about her career all of a sudden, she wondered. However, trying to brush away those thoughts, she replied, "I am waiting for their final guidelines for the competition. Once they send that to me, I can start preparing accordingly."

Aakaash heard her quietly and carefully. He replied, "That makes sense."

As they spoke, Tiasha parked the car in the humungous parking street near India Gate, which was already occupied by many cars. While locking the doors, she asked, "How about your work? I haven't seen anything significant happening in the few days. Or perhaps—"

She stopped.

Her expression narrated very well the story of her mindset, which Aakaash read without any words. He said, as they walked towards the silence of the huge lush grounds, "What happened?"

Tiasha looked sombre this time. Realising that whatever happened the morning could not just be his fault, she said, "Or... perhaps, I had started being so indifferent towards you that I stopped bothering about what's going on in your life!"

Aakaash smiled. Yes, he felt this was a reason, yes he didn't feel he was solely responsible and yes, he did want her to realise this. One part of his subconscious wanted her to apologise and pamper his ego, and the other side wanted him to be a comforting buddy to Tiasha. He could have easily chosen the first one and made her feel guilty, made her upset and now that she was kneeling down, make her kneel down and rise in ego. But, he chose the second option. He said, putting his arms around her neck and walking, "You know what?"

Tiasha gave him a blank look. She was now in a 'self-critique' mode. Aakaash continued, as he brought their favourite ice cream, Choco Bar. Unwrapping it and giving the ice cream to her, he said, "We are like the choices we make. Whenever we go to an ice cream parlour, both of us always have the option of getting the fanciest ice creams, *haina?* But, at the end, we choose our favourite and the simplest choco bar. Why? Have you ever wondered?"

Tiasha replied, "Because I love eating this and not those fancy ones."

"Exactly my point. You and I are exactly the same. We are happiest when we are knitted in a simple bond of friendship. Yes, we have feelings for each other, which I am sure we value, but being in a relationship is perhaps not meant for us. See, I like spending time with my partner, you like spending time with your best friend and the expectations that we have from our partners become way different. But, when we are like this – the way we are right now – we feel really comfortable."

"Yes, exactly Aakaash! I feel elated when I don't have the burden of proving myself to be a good partner. I feel free then."

Aakaash smiled. He had correctly decoded her mindset this time as well. He was really proud of the fact that he knew her inside out. He said, "Then let's be free rather than being complicated. The biggest mistake we were making was to hold each other back, which we never did as buddies. Let's just be those buddies to each other where we live for the dreams we see and the vision we look forward to. Let's fall, get up and then fall and then get up; we can be with each other and help the other one get up, but let's at least try and let each other fall if that's what our career demands."

Tiasha heard him carefully and forgetting whatever happened, gave him a tight hug.

He smiled. This hug had the trust that she always possessed for him. Her heartbeats once again assured him of the fulfilment of his dream and her strength was no longer his weakness. Once again, they sorted the entangled thread of their lives and silently took apart the relationship which was distancing two people madly in love – but in denial, again!

Brilliantly made quesadillas!

Advertising is one field which is a combination of all – from creating storyboards on paper to directing the actors to pose in a particular way to getting everything released to the client. It probably needs everything a person can invest in, especially if he is working as a creative head of a team.

For Tiasha, the Choko Majista ad was the first one that she was working on and when I say the first one, it means handling everything alone, without any supervision. Of course, Anushi helped her with the basic information and guidelines, but it was she who had to work on the project and deliver it to the client.

Though she had spent two months in office, she was still adjusting to the new environment. If you keep a plant in an altogether new environment, it takes time in adapting to the surroundings, doesn't it? *Toh, agar kabhi fass jao na* and you feel you don't know anything – *galtiya zyada badh jaaye* and office becomes troublesome, *padhai na ho, pressure zyada badh jaaye* – say three words to yourself. It is okay!

For Tiasha, the first challenge was to meet tight deadlines. Advertising has quick turnaround time for digital ads and Tiasha's first ad was delayed by a few days.

She had worked diligently on the project and had honestly invested a lot of hours of genuine hard work. However, due to dependencies on the cross-functional teams, the delay was evidently visible. Mohit said, while he took the meeting, "Tiasha, we are running very late on your ad. It's a digital ad and the company does not pay us enough for you to take an entire month on it. The turnaround time for it is ten days."

Tiasha hated him for a millisecond. How could someone be so rude to her, she questioned herself. But, ended up replying, "I agree, Mohit. But everything is clear from my end; it's just the media which is pending with the media developers."

Mohit responded almost immediately, "You are leading a team of different cross-functional teams. Nothing is clear from your end till you deliver the advert. It's your ad and you have brought it so far. So learn to take responsibility."

Tiasha nodded with a sombre expression on her face. Everyone in the team could see that. However, Tiasha knew that Mohit made sense. She did not hate him like she did a moment ago. She rather registered one statement in her head, "It's your project and you are responsible for it."

♌

She quickly came out of the meeting and sat with the media developers to expedite the process. The developer said, "I'll do this by tomorrow only. I don't have bandwidth for this work today."

Had Tiasha been herself, she would have given him a sound thrashing, but she was extremely calm. She replied, "The delivery date is day after tomorrow. How can we keep the project with us for seven days and still say that it would take two more days? We have to close the media part today. Park it to the animation team by end of the day. We can't deviate from this."

Varun replied, "You kids don't teach us how to work. Go and tell Mohit that we won't be able to meet the client delivery date."

Ego – the killing force of every relation. And, this situation isn't new when the experienced minds deny listening to the newcomers. Happens everywhere, doesn't it?

Tiasha kept calm and replied peacefully, with a smile. She was extremely humble. "*Sir, jaaega toh ye project date par hi.* If you can do it, it's fine, else I'll ask Mohit to align another resource to it. Just write it over an email. I'll handle the rest."

She smiled and walked away. Varun cribbed about her way of speaking and working, but all Tiasha cared about at that moment was her ad. She had to deliver her first ad on time. She came back to her workstation and sat with stress doing *bhangra* on her forehead. Anushi saw her forehead sweating profusely and her expressions overwhelmed with stress.

Anushi told her, "Tiasha, work hard but do not work under stress; you'll end up making blunders. Relax and then work."

Tiasha smiled and replied, "Yes Captain. I am fine."

Anushi replied, "Do you want to come over for a coffee or tea to take a break? We can go out for a few minutes."

Tiasha reverted, still focussing most on her desktop, "No Captain. I'll be fine. I have to close this."

Anushi smiled, knowing the fact that she would not get up, even if god came and told her to come with him to heaven. *Such a workaholic she was.*

Tiasha kept taking quick statuses of her project from Varun and then the animators. She literally sat with them throughout the day and throughout the night to get the animation completed. Yes, you read it right, without any exaggeration that she stayed back throughout the night and kept all the animators in office too.

ᘓ

Next morning, in the meeting, Tiasha knew Mohit would sarcastically ask her about the progress of the project. She was pretty much prepared for a good round of sarcasm. However, to her surprise, he didn't turn up for the meeting. The meeting, therefore, was led by Anushi. She said, "Good job, girl! Closing a project as extensively animated as this one in one day takes guts."

Tiasha smiled. Anisha, her closest team-mate looked at her and congratulated her through her happy eyes.

Tiasha came out smiling. She joked while taking her place, "When I don't work, he's proudly here to shower his sarcasm on me and when I have been here there the whole day and whole night, he hardly bothers. Uff, the bosses."

Anisha looked at her and smiled. Tiasha and her cribbing were two inseparable lovers. Like a little kid, whenever she had something to crib about, she would walk up to Anisha and blabber everything out. *Coincidently, or perhaps not that coincidently, a person with the same name became the person I always walk up to whenever anything happens. I remember, recently I had got a good thrashing for not writing a mail properly. I was humiliated by letting everyone around know that I made a mistake and I didn't say a single word. I had made a mistake, I heard for it.*

However, feeling shattered, I remember I have bothered Anisha with my tears every second day. I had actually become a cry baby and that cry baby always walked up to her Cancerian partner to find solace. And every time I narrated a story, Anisha was there next to me – to scold me when required and to give me a tight hug to calm me down when she felt there was need to console me.

Well, in Tiasha's life too, Anisha played the same crucial role. She smiled seeing her excitement to complete a project. Anushi and Anisha both knew this was one of the most ambitious projects and Mohit had deliberately given it to Tiasha to test her patience, while juggling between delivering quality work within stringent timelines. Luckily, Tiasha had passed the test.

They laughed and happily enjoyed with her. Meanwhile, Anushi asked, "Tiasha, is our advert signed off?"

Tiasha smiled as she nodded positively. Anushi replied, "Great. I am releasing the final version to the client then."

Tiasha smiled as she saw her first advert being released. Anushi too was happy to release a project which not only had hard work and zeal, but also genuine positivity and innocence. Meanwhile, while Mohit sat in his cabin and read the release mail, he confirmed her potential, 'She did it. Good work, Tiasha. Much against my expectations, though.'

Judgmental since day one, Mohit had taken Tiasha to be a carefree and careless teenager. Being highly experienced and professional, he felt she was too kiddish to be given responsibilities. However, proving him wrong was one victory which Tiasha achieved. *He never judged her creativity, though.*

Being himself, he did not appreciate her or any of her efforts. He just sent a mail asking all the team members to come for dinner.

Tiasha quipped, "What's this dinner for?"

Anushi smiled and said, "You could assume it is for you."

Tiasha smiled as they went for dinner.

Has it ever happened with you that you worked really hard on either a college event or a school function and at the end, when everyone thought that the event was over and considered the day had ended, you sat down and gulped the silence after the turbulent few days of your life? That *sukoon wali* feeling is worth all the hard work. And... when your work gives you that *sukoon, aur kya chahiye fir?*

As they sat on the dinner table, Tiasha saw a different side of Mohit; he joked and spoke happily. Tiasha had never seen him that chilled out. Perhaps the corporate world makes you like that – a stern boss in office and trying to be a cool boss at professionally unprofessional dinners. *Whatever little I know about the corporate world, I just know that no party is unofficial, no get together is personal. That's why it's always important to be in your senses.*

Tiasha observed the culture around her. She was never this formal, she realised and smiled to herself.

While munching the delicious quesadillas, Tiasha said, "Have this Anishu, it tastes so good."

Quesadilla is a Mexican dish prepared by stuffing crispy veggies in white sauce inside a wheat wrap. While they ate it, Tiasha wondered, how similar her life was to those quesadillas. Just like them, she had been boiled in the stressful white sauce and just like them, she was proud to have come out to be successful.

Isn't life similar to cooking? If, at the end of the day, you can prepare a dish worth cherishing, everything starts seeming beautiful. Similar is with life, if you can cherish each day spent, good or bad, at the end, you'll love cooking it.

Chocolate brownie!

If you know me, you would know by now that I have a sweet tooth. (The one bigger than an elephant's.)

No matter how full I am, I will happily have a dessert at the end of a meal, and that too, twice my capacity. Just recently, while travelling to Indore, when I was just strolling around the airport, I found the love of my life – chocolate brownies. Within two minutes, I had ordered and devoured a whole brownie.

And as I ate like a monster, I spotted a lovely couple sitting next to me. On the comfortable Starbucks chairs, they sat and happily shared a brownie. For a moment, I was mesmerized by their bond. I wanted to have a person beside me as well. I wanted to share my brownie as well. I wanted… Just then, I realised I had you guys to share stories with. The workaholic me told me, "work!" And happily enough, I turned to the love of my life, my laptop and completed Tiasha's story!

P.S.: Too much information without reason, eh? As my Metro buddy calls it, 'good to know information', which can easily be ignored, but the way I speak, I am sure, no one can ignore.

♌

Chalo finally, work was in place now!

"Trust me Tiasha, I want to tie the apron around you when you stand there to become India's best chefs," Aakaash said as they stood face to face in a crowded Metro. He was in Gurgaon for some work and while coming back, he chose to wait for an hour so that he could get some time with his best friend. Tiasha, on the other hand, quickly wrapped up all her work, knowing that Aakaash was waiting for her. *Doesn't it happen? When someone waits for you, your priority is to reach to them. And whenever someone waits for you, I have always believed that they wait because they really care for you, because everyone has a choice of leaving. Always!*

As they boarded an extremely crowded Metro from Huda City Centre, Aakaash discussed a lot about his stand-up career and the challenges he was facing. He did get some offers for promotions, but it was a tiff between his creativity and the producer's money. Neither of them wanted to back off. But, at least, his channel was becoming so popular that ad producers wanted to feature him; that was something he had been waiting for and that was something he had wished desperately for.

After completing his tale of comedy, making her laugh endlessly, narrating even the most complicated situations in the easiest manner possible, Aakaash finally spoke to her about her career and the World Food Festival which was coming up very soon. It certainly would be a life-changing experience for her, he knew.

Tiasha replied, "Just hope I reach there on time," she said wryly.

"What do you mean?" he asked immediately.

"I still have two months to serve in Apticon before I can resign, Aakaash, and I don't want to end up being a quitter. I want to fight on," she started, but was abruptly interrupted.

"What is wrong with you? Just for the sake of being stubborn, I will not let you miss this opportunity. Even you know that you'll meet the best people in the circuit and working under Rajiv and

Nimisha, you mentioned yourself, would enhance your skills as well. Then why do you need to stay on here when there's a path already built by you, for you. Walk on it, Tiyu."

Alright, let me introduce Rajiv and Nimisha. They are the mentors who would be staying with the participants for a month and would train them for the competitions. Rajiv Tondon was one of the youngest and most successful chefs that India had. He had been the face of the cooking shows on leading channels and acquired enough expertise to be at the top at the age of just twenty-nine.

Tiasha was already a huge fan of his recipes as she saw novelty in most of them. She loved people who didn't stay at one place and looked ahead to climb the ladder of success. *Nomadic herders, maybe. Or wanderers!*

The second chef was Nishima Kapoor, another big name in the culinary industry. She was the author of twenty-seven cook books and knew enough to guide the lot of aspiring chefs. Tiasha knew this for a fact that being under them would take her places. Aakaash had just reiterated that fact.

Tiasha said, "I know that. I really want to be there, but I also like my job. I get to learn, I get a reason to come here and work every day. Yes, I face challenges; yes, I face the dire need to leave the organisation when a client feedback comes in and is negative. I agree, I want to just leave everything and go on a vacation to de-stress myself. But, I never want to quit something mid-way."

"Tiasha, stop being kiddish. They appreciate you because your work is good. They give you reasons because they want a hard working employee and if you are talking about trust…it's the corporate world. I hope you know that? Your company pampers you because they see potential in you for building their company. Do not think you are indispensible for them. You are just a small fish in a big ocean. One employee less will not make a big difference to Apticon. *Band nahi ho jaegi company tere chhod dene se.*"

"I—" Tiasha tried interrupting, but was stopped right there.

"Let me complete. One employee less, no difference. One chef less from the world, a lot of difference. Act mature if you can and think before taking decisions," he completed.

As the Metro stopped at Qutub Minar, a traffic junction, a lot of people entered, pushing the crowd inside. Seeing that, Aakaash took a step back and made space for Tiasha to stand near him. He never told her, but since ever, he knew he was taking care of a child. It wasn't as if he was protecting her, he was just being mature with a kid around.

Sometimes, some people speak less, express almost negligibly but at the end of the day, they are those people who would go beyond their limits to help you out. Never would they say they care, but if you have the right eyes, you'll see through their silence and realise how much do they care, silently.

He said, when he didn't see Tiasha walking a step towards the free space he created for her,

"*Ye jagah maine Qutub Minar banana ke liye nahi ki hai.*"

Sweet, she felt.

As they stood inches away from each other, Tiasha raised her eyes and saw directly in his, and that very moment, she wanted to take a step ahead and give him a tight hug.

She was exhausted and felt like putting her head on him and sleeping peacefully as they stood, knowing the fact that serenity lied there. She knew if she just held his arms and peacefully slept on his shoulders, the confusions in her mind would come to rest at once; she knew if she just held his hand while they walked, she would find solace; and she knew that just giving him a tight hug, putting her head on him and staying there for a minute would bring peace back to her.

She knew she was seeking peace, she knew she was desperately looking for tranquillity in him and the funny fact was that she knew that she would get that tranquillity. Aakaash wouldn't mind being there. Just that, things had gone from '*It's complicated*' to '*Just friends*' and letting her feelings do what they wanted, Tiasha was afraid she would lose her best friend, once again.

'After such difficulties, things have simplified. I can't afford to complicate them,' she reminded herself.

Coming back on herself, she thought and replied, "But, don't you think being stubborn and leaving office is unprofessional?"

"Then, don't you think that being a chef, who could do wonders in her culinary career, staying in an advertising company is unprofessional too?"

The confidence with which Aakaash assured her was delivering odes about his trust in her profession.

Many times, there would be people who wouldn't tell you on your face how much they value your dreams, but they do. I am sure you have that one friend too!

Finally, the friends were back. Their conversations were back to being about career and work, replacing and throwing the pampering away. Thank god, else, it was really funny looking at the two of them!

Making her much more confident of her cooking career and discussing work, they reached home. Of course, laughter and smiles accompanied them. Tiasha always wondered how Aakaash got her laughing on each and every thing around them. Even if she was angry, he could make her smile for no good reason and once she smiled, Aakaash would just not let the anger come back. She knew she couldn't hide the smile when he was around.

Every time, every moment and every day, whenever she cribbed, he gave her full freedom to crib so that all her frustration ended before she entered her kitchen. Every day, whenever office was difficult, Aakaash gave her the strength to fight. Once he created a new problem, she would forget the old one and focus on cooking. He would make nasty comments so that she started dealing with them there and faced lesser difficulties when she went to Mahabaleshwar. And he stayed firm even when she would be dicey. It wasn't patriarchal support, it wasn't to prove that he was stronger than her, it was just support which kept him going as well. He just innocently liked being next to her and her innocent laughter added to his achievements!

Personally, I can never be this giving that you forget yourself and keep the other person above you. But, Aakaash did, honestly and diligently.

As Tiasha lay on her bed that night, tameless thoughts about her career disturbed her. It seemed as if she was between a web of entangled thoughts. It seemed as if each thought was pushing and pulling her priorities, each thought was pushing her inside the well of confusions. She felt emotionally drained and mentally frozen.

She did not want to add a tag of being a quitter to her life's story; nor did she want to quit on her dreams. Therefore, choosing one was a tough decision, but at some point or the other, that decision had to be taken. *Kab tak bhagoge yaar,* you will have to take that leap.

Being a fresh lime soda

Sitting at Bronx – the Bar Exchange, Gurgaon – on the occasion of a friend's birthday, I looked confused and puzzled. The waiter asked, "What would you like to have, ma'am?"

I looked at the menu for beverages and acted as if I understood everything, but in reality, I got nothing. The menu had names of drinks which I had never heard of. It seemed as if Alice was lost in the wonderland of beverages, beer, and champagnes. Do you remember how Mario felt in between the lost lands? I felt exactly that I don't drink and I'd apparently be the last person going to dimly-lit places. I feel slightly suffocated in there. *Toh bhaiya, hume toh kuch bhi nahi pata tha.*

Trying to play it safe, I just said, "Fresh lime soda."

He then asked, "Ok ma'am. Sweet or salty?"

The tricky question here. I loved sweet and I loved salty too. They both had distinguished tastes, so how could I choose one?

'What should I choose' I asked myself as I just made an impulsive decision, getting embarrassed by the waiter's glance and said, "Mixed."

ℓ

Just like the situation I was in while choosing between sweet and salty, Tiasha was in a situation where she had to choose between her professional growth and her passion. Rather than quitting, she had decided on taking the torturous path. The previous night, she decided to break the news to her immediate supervisors. She spoke to Mohit and Anushi and applied for a one month leave.

Replying to which, Mohit asked, "How long have you been in office, Tiasha?"

Sarcasm at its best. Honestly, Tiasha did expect such nasty comments from him; he was used to saying those, after all.

"Tiasha, when I joined office, I worked like you. I worked like a donkey – day and night and that helped me become who I am."

Tiasha spoke in between, as Anushi listened to their conversation quietly, "I agree Mohit, but this is what I live for."

"But, this is not something that gives you a living, child. At twenty-one, I understand you feel extremely ambitious. But why risk your stability for something which will have nothing in store for you, except a void?" he replied.

Tiasha answered, "I have made up my mind, Mohit. I really want this leave, else I will still choose my passion."

For the first time, there was a stubborn sparkle in Tiasha's eyes. Remember the first time, in the interview when Naina asked her what was she doing to meet her goals, Tiasha was apprehensive because she herself had no answer to that question. She did want to achieve something, but how, even she didn't know. It wasn't as if she had no dream or no ambition then, but today she had a determination to achieve that goal. For a change, she wasn't that confused.

Mohit read her expression. With the years of experience he had, he could see through her perseverance and he knew saying anything wouldn't influence her now. He knew if she could stick to her official work day and night, she will definitely put her life in building her dream.

He replied, calmly, "See Tiasha, on a personal note, I would not like to leave an employee like you, who has apparently learnt triple the amount the others of your batch have. I can see a difference in the working style that you have and I love to see you working so hard.

At the same time, being practical, I can't stop myself from showing the mirror to you. Honestly, your passion will not return ten lakhs a year to you, will it?"

Tiasha was quiet. Mohit continued, understanding that he got a way to her mind.

"I suggest take some time, Tiasha. Think if your competition, which you are not even sure of winning, will be worth risking your job for. At the end of the day, it is just a competition."

Tiasha didn't say anything. She just went into a thoughtful zone, pondering upon what Mohit said. She knew Mohit had a lot of experience and his views mattered to her. The tricky part was that Mohit knew this as well.

The corporate world is apparently not a place to be emotional and be attached. Yes, there are many good people whom you should admire and adore. Yes, there are many seniors whom you would like to get influenced by. Yes, there are many reasons to stay there, but there's one reason that can fight all those reasons to go out and if you have that reason, follow that. *Kyunki,* trust me, every time you would want to swim in the tumultuous ocean, your well wishers would try and keep you safe, but you know what? You really have to get out of that safe zone to shine as a winner.

Personally, I had one friend who would always tell me to take the most difficult path. If Path A was easy, he would deliberately throw me on to Path B, which was full of challenges. Initially, I hated him for not pampering me. I was pretty used to the pampering, after all. But, at the end of every argument, I would see a reason why he behaved with me in a strict way. I would see a logical reason about his decisions. Sometimes, it was difficult for an impulsive person like me to understand how logic worked every time. I quipped and asked him as well but never got an answer. He perhaps wanted me to find that answer myself.

You know, when everyone told me getting appreciated at work was great and they were busy congratulating me, he told me, "Appreciate the appreciation, but do not take decisions because of this appreciation. Keep your priorities sorted."

I was annoyed at his art of never motivating me, but in reality that was the exact motivation I needed to complete this book. I realise as I complete *our* book that perhaps, we all need such friends who could keep us grounded to reality and our dreams! Especially in offices – if you work, you would know that you spend almost twelve hours a day working with stress dancing on your forehead and in those twelve hours, you need people like this stupid friend of mine to keep you grounded, whom you'll always call stupid, but thank at the end of the day.

Therefore, even when some people flatter you to make you go ahead with appreciation, I would say, stay grounded and stay in the company of those who can keep you grounded.

Tiasha, yes, coming back to her, she was confused. As being confused was her forte, she came out of the meeting, hassled.

Just like the confused me while I was choosing between the sweet and salty fresh lime soda, Tiasha was too at the verge of choosing the option of 'mixed'.

Mixed fresh lime soda – on the one hand it gives you the taste of both sweet and salty, and on the other, you are to be devoid of having any one taste completely. It perhaps can work when you are happy to be moderate. The question then was, was Tiasha happy being a moderate? Could she be satisfied with having fifty percent of her dream come true?

Perfect fits, if they were

Tiasha came home, confused and with tons of questions brewing like coffee in water. And that was the exact reason that without turning to the right and entering her house, she pressed the door bell of the flat opposite to hers.

She entered and greeted everyone in Aakaash's house. On the one hand, where he hardly spoke to anyone at his place, she gushed a breeze of positivity as she entered his house. She spoke to his parents, chatted a bit with his grandparents and then turned to Vaishnavi's room.

The youngest member of Aakaash's house and the most pampered friend that Tiasha had. It was actually funny to see a pampered kid pampering another one, but Tiasha felt mature when she was with Vaishnavi. She felt responsible and she tried her best to behave in a mature manner. Not having any sibling, she saw Vaishnavi as one for sure. (Sounds too Rajshree movie-ish, I know.)

Anyway, as she was just about to barge inside, she saw Aakaash inside and hence, she stopped immediately. There was a conversation which she didn't want to interrupt. Vaishnavi said, looking upset, "What's the point in getting such lovely dresses for me when I don't even get to wear them, bhaiya."

Aakaash had secretly ordered a few dresses from her wishlist. He knew his mom and dad would never get her those and hence, being the pampering brother that he was, he had bought them with his savings, which generally was the case. In fact, whenever I looked at Aakaash, I always felt he'd be a great parent – that's what parenting is, after all – when you pamper and scold at the same time, when no grudges stay and when conversations are crystal clear. Aakaash never tried to intrude in his sister's life; he rather believed that if she felt like sharing anything, she would approach him herself. He had created their bond to be an open resort to her, where she could walk up whenever she wanted to. He never insisted that she share something with him.

Many a times, he could evidently guess that something was wrong with her but didn't interfere in her life; he gave her the space to find answers to her questions, to know how she wanted to solve problems and how she would want to handle situations. And in the course of this, if she fell, he was always there to help her get up.

Just like every time, he sat by her side on the football bean bag that these siblings had in their room. Comfortably sitting with his legs folded and putting his phone on silent, he asked, "Who told you not to wear these?"

Vaishnavi explained, "No one. It is just the gaze of so many people that makes me uncomfortable. Being strong and independent, you always told me to fight people myself, but how do I fight with those silent, uncomfortable glances?"

Aakaash heard her carefully, after which he said, "*Bachche,* listen to me."

Whenever he had something to explain, he generally would always start this way. And whenever he spoke to Vaishnavi, there was a unique innocence on his face, which I believe was exclusively for her. That innocence in his eyes and that priceless smile contained an equal amount of concern and affection for his sister. It was evident that Aakaash was a different Aakaash when he was with his sister.

You know, I am the eldest sibling of three little monsters – Gungun, Bhai and Soumya. All three of them are a notch higher than each other when it comes to being naughty. And the best part is that since the day these three were born, I received three best friends. It was almost as if I would never leave my Bua and Mami because I always wanted to stay close to these kids. Today, when we are growing up together, I learn from them and they have taught me much more than words can say. There's no word like cousin. I believe it's the only word a dictionary cannot define. So, I do get the feeling of being the mature one around them too. Although they feel they are the ones driving me ahead, which by the way is true!

That's the bond siblings have, that's the bond that keeps them bonded together!

Aakaash quickly simplified things in his mind and explained, "See, you cannot go and change the mindset of the people gazing at you, but you cannot also let their gaze affect your decisions, can you?"

"I know I can't, bhai, but the gaze is discomforting. We talk about being open and independent, but at the end, I think what mom says is correct – to keep yourself safe by hiding every bit of your body."

Irritation was evidently visible on Vaishanvi's face and that perturbed Aakaash. Tiasha could see that clearly, but she knew Aakaash would handle her and not let her give in to such thoughts and hence she silently watched him.

She was right.

He said, "Yes, mom is right. But, partially. You should be safe, that's true. But, not by letting go of your wishes. Just be aware. Also, think about whom you are going out with. If it's parents, then you could be yourself as you know you have that bubble of protection around you. Even if you are with trusted friends, it's cool. And even if you are alone, that's okay if the place is fine. Just be cautious when you know the place is slightly tricky. What's the problem, then?"

Vaishnavi heard him quietly. Whenever her mind was not at peace, she knew her brother was her fire brigade. Aakaash continued, "Just be aware and keep your eyes and ears open. And, even you know, I'm telling this to you not because you are a girl but even for myself. Do you think I don't need to be aware? I am equally at risk as you are, and I want you to handle that situation all by yourself. And if need be, for me too. That's the reason I tie a rakhi on your wrist too, right?"

Vaishnavi nodded as Aakaash continued, "See, I am always a call away, but I want you to be so strong that you handle situations yourself. And for that, make your mind strong. You have to be brave so that such morons don't affect your mental peace."

She smiled a bit as she nodded again. Aakaash said, now to lighten the mood a bit, "You must be thinking that bhaiya keeps lecturing me all the time and that whenever I talk to him, he just bothers me with deep thoughts and words..."

Hearing this, Vaishnavi did not even let him complete and gave him a tight hug. She said, "You are world's best brother. *Best se bhi best, bhaiya.*"

Tiasha saw them together and smiled. Such was their relationship. Aakaash never held the strings of her freedom and yet was knitting her decisions by his suggestions. He advised her when he felt so and let her be free to take her own decisions otherwise. After all, he wanted Vaishnavi to make her life, and not him. But, he made sure he was around when she was struggling – not to reduce the stress but to pump more strength in her to face anything and everything with a smile.

Knowing this fact, Tiasha for once wanted to join their hug and tell Aakaash how undoubtedly different he was. Silently, she was inspired with the way he was with Vaishnavi, and she just felt like telling this to him. But just when she was about to do so, Vaishnavi said, "I am jealous of Aashna. She's lucky to have such a good boyfriend."

Tiasha did not feel very happy hearing this name. How come Aakaash had a girl in his life she didn't know about?

Well, jealousy. She didn't like to even hear a mention of someone else in his life, but at the same time, she didn't want to take that place in his life too. God only knows what she wanted. However, pretty much a trait of Tiasha. And unlike Aakaash, she was expressive of what she felt.

Meanwhile Aakaash replied to Vaishnavi, "She isn't my girlfriend. Just a fan who likes me. My first fan who thought I was worth having a crush on!"

That pierced Tiasha again. Had Aakaash not been serious, he would have told Vaishanvi to shut up with a taut face. But rather, he blushed. Reacting to which, Tiasha entered and fuming, she said, "Congratulations. Now I know why you are so busy."

Throwing a pillow on the bed and bubbling with anger, she left aggressively. Aakaash and Vaishnavi silently looked at her walking back. Vaishnavi smiled looking at both of her favourite people. She just said, "Go and handle her. Since she is so angry, *kitchen me hogi wo.*"

Aakaash nodded but looked disappointed. Although he walked towards the kitchen, his mind was stuck at the girl Vaishnavi just spoke about.

Aashna was one of the fans who had stalked Aakaash a bit on YouTube and managed to meet him a day before. She had met him and immediately, going on her knees, proposed to him. A timid and petite face, blinking and blazing eyes, smoothened hair and exactly the make-up that she needed – she was really beautiful. And without talking too much, I'd rather say that Aakaash was attracted to her.

As he walked up to Tiasha's house, as expected, she was in the kitchen, but wasn't able to manage anything. The pan of milk was overflowing, the vegetables that she had put on the stove were half-burnt and the flour she was preparing looked ruined as well. Tiasha was very complicated and Aakaash knew it. He knew how her brain worked. If his brain took the highway to reach his destination, her way would take the most complicated path of all.

She had feelings but would never acknowledge those. He had feelings too, but he did not want those feelings to come between her dream and her. At the same time, he didn't want her to come between his career and him. He knew if he stayed with her, he would end up affecting himself more than anyone else because he genuinely loved her and that was the sole reason he considered moving on. He knew he wouldn't love anyone as much as he loved her.

He was actually angry at the way Tiasha was behaving. He wanted to leave her then and there, to handle everything that she faced, all by herself. But, she had a discomforting expression on her face, which he couldn't bear.

♌

He walked inside the kitchen and stood next to Tiasha. While he wanted to argue, he simply kept quiet and looked at an annoyed Tiasha. You know, when some people would feel bad, they would be angry and they would really be irritated, but they have a magical strength to hide everything inside their little heart and still pretend to be mature and would never even say a single word. Aakaash was that person. Yes, he felt dejected when things didn't work between him and Tiasha, but he wrapped that sadness under his ambition. Not once would you see him being affected, even when wounds inside his heart were fresh and sensitive.

Even today, he was frustrated by the way she always reacted. It was as if only Tiasha felt bad and he was, well, heartless. He felt there were too many expectations from him. Today, he felt taken for granted. However, he just stood by her calmly.

Not even looking at him and fighting with the flour in the plate, Tiasha sternly said, "Go and talk to your girlfriend. Let me work."

Aakaash smiled and replied, "I can very well see how the work is going on."

Tiasha looked around and seeing her kitchen in such a mess, she started crying, venting out her frustration. She kneeled down as she said, "I feel really irritated, Aakaash. I am unable to take a decision. Whether I should take a leap or stay here and earn more in office? I love both, my work and my passion. And then, I am really afraid of letting you go away. How do you think I am gonna manage everything?"

A tear dropped down her cheek as she sat on her kitchen floor. Aakaash knew her feelings. He knew she was going through a lot of dilemmas and accepting the fact that he wanted to move on was certainly too much for her. He sat down and taking her in his arms, he explained, "*Accha* relax. Shh. Tell me, what is the problem in office?"

Tiasha cried like a baby. She was one, at times. And confusion was something she lived with, and got irritated with. It wasn't her fault; there were too many things going on in a short span of time for her. She had a competition around the corner from which she expected a leap in her culinary career, then there was office which was teaching her a lot, and there was Aakaash, whom she could see sailing away from her. Like the milk on the stove, her emotions were overflowing; like her vegetables which were overheated, her patience too was overheated; and like her kitchen, even her mind was messed up.

Aakaash embraced her back as she kept her head on his chest and wrapped her arms around him. She found solace there. She said, "I feel confused. I have two options – to choose between office and my passion. I don't know what I should choose? I don't want to quit, Aakaash. Neither do I want to forego the competition, else I'll regret it throughout my life. I am stuck between these two choices."

Aakaash stroked her hair and replied, "If you would ask me, I'd say take your dream and don't think about being a quitter. But, I know you will regret it the minute you leave either of the two right now. So, you need to be very sure before taking this decision. Didn't Uncle and Aunty say the same thing to you?"

Yes, her parents had told her exactly the same thing. She actually wondered how Aakaash and they were pretty much always on the same page. She didn't say anything, but just hid herself in his embrace. Like always, she felt as if he was her ozone layer, who protected her emotionally.

Aakaash said, after a brief pause, "You know what? When life is giving you two choices, create the third choice. Do what you want and not choose from the choices that life is throwing at you."

"How?" she quipped.

To which, he smiled and replied, "That you will figure out. So that you miss your best friend a little less. And stop smoking, Tiasha. This is the last time I am warning you."

For the first time, Aakaash didn't spoon-feed her. He asked her to find her path. How else would he reduce the dependency she had on him? And how else would he limit her effect in his life?

He might not openly accept, but he still had feelings for her, which had a to and fro in his mind and it became difficult for him to live with them. Being himself, he didn't say a single word, but rather was trying to walk away. He felt moving on would help him *move on*. He really thought so?

You know the biggest problem with some people is that they want to create an image of themselves as the simplest human beings, pretending they never get affected or they are the most satisfied, but in actuality, they are the ones who need to be nurtured the most, pampered the most. They might not want to express this openly, but observing them closely would prove this to you!

Anyway, Tiasha smiled and Aakaash smiled back, wiping her tears.

He said, as they got up, "Trust me, your friend is all yours. Whenever you need Aakaash, you are my priority. I just want you to understand the fact that even I need someone to walk up to. Aashna and I are not dating, okay? But, we might. I feel we are similar and are on the same page. So, just throw the fear away that I'll change; we are the same. Okay?"

Tiasha nodded, not convincingly though. Aakaash gave her a hug and left for his place. He knew it was difficult for her, but it was what was right for both of them. He knew she would face difficulties dealing with the strict attitude that he had taken. Never had he ever left her while she was this sad, rather he would take every possible measure to pamper her. But today, he wanted her to take that pain of figuring out her solutions.

And, as I write so, do not mistake Tiasha to be a damsel in distress who needed a prince to protect her. She could take care of herself. It was just the emotional support that comforted her. And I have always believed that we are dependent on people only if we let ourselves be dependent on them. It certainly is not true that we are dependent because we don't have options or we are weaker. But he reason is simple; you want to walk along. Not that we can't handle things ourselves, it's just that letting yourself get affected by someone is a choice and it's a risk you don't take with everyone, right?

Tiasha had a gush of emotional melodrama happening in her mind as she turned around after locking her door, and he rang the bell and said, "I want to tie the apron around India's best chef one day. Prove me right."

Saying so, he winked and left, imprinting these words on her mind.

Margarita

Whenever I travel through Terminal 1 of the Indira Gandhi International Airport, there's a fixed schedule that I follow. I straight away go to Pizza Hut and order cheese garlic bread with a Coke. Over the years, I put on weight, my taste buds grew fonder of other delights, I grew crazier and many other things changed, but my menu did not. Just like some habits which are so stubborn that they refuse to leave you even when you want to leave them behind.

Just last time while I was travelling to Indore, while I ordered the garlic bread with cheese, I saw on the other side of the counter a familiar face – Rajkishore. He has been there behind the computer taking orders diligently since all these years. I greeted him and while waiting for my garlic bread to arrive, I saw Rajkishore pack a margarita for a little kid.

I asked, being myself,

"*Kaun hi ye sirf cheese ka pizza khata hoga, bhaiya?*"

He replied, smiling, "*Madam, ye toh dekhne ka tareeka hai.* Perspectives."

For a minute, I couldn't help but judge myself to be so irrelevant. Everyone has their own set of choices and to judge them is not something really cool. In a fraction of a moment, I felt guilty. That kid might enjoy the pizza, but just because I did not like it, I happily concluded that it was boring.

ℓ

Just the way I judged margarita-lovers, Tiasha was being judged for her choices when she firmly put forward her view in front of Mohit, Naina, Anushi and the HR guy. Resolving the confusions and the dilemmas that she had, she finally took a stand for her dream. Finally! *Warna main soch rahi thi ki agle janam me hi madam solve kar paati apne confusions!*

She had written a formal mail to her supervisors asking them to meet her over a discussion and help her resolve her concerns.

When she sat in front of all four pairs of eyes, she felt nervous. However, she had chosen her flavour, remember?

She started, "Hi everyone and thank you for coming here to this meeting. I had some serious choices to make a week ago when I first discussed it with my team leads. And after thinking for more than thirty hours, I have come to a conclusion where I want to achieve my dreams. Cooking is my passion and living my passion is my choice. I wouldn't lie, but for once, I was inclined towards the idea of staying here and getting a lump sum salary hike. But, at the end, my heart won. I will go to the competition.

"As you may already know, there is a month-long competition in Mahabaleshwar and I want to accelerate my cooking career by taking part in it. I have decided I will go to Mahabaleshwar.

"I have asked for this meeting so that I could figure out any possible way of getting a leave for a month. I can come back and work double the hours maybe.

"And, this is not because I am attracted towards my salary, no. It's because quitting doesn't suit Tiasha."

As she spoke, Mohit nodded disappointedly. He did not want to lose a resource which was both creative and hardworking, and insanely crazy for work.

At the same time, he did not want to start a trend of giving month-long holidays. He really thought that he had retained her when he had spoken to her and he had been successful in making her decisions seem dicey to her. *Corporate kathayein* – there's nothing wrong with it too, I believe!

Naina looked disappointed, but she was happy too. She could see that confident spark in Tiasha's eyes today, which had been missing all these months. Anushi, perhaps was the only one who was the happiest. She didn't care about her team or her office at that moment; all she cared was for Tiasha's dreams.

However, the HR guy said, "See Tiasha, it is not possible for us to give such a long leave. I am afraid you will then have to make a permanent choice between your passion and your career."

"Then, I am afraid I have already made my choice," Tiasha replied immediately with a smile on her face. She was kind of expecting the answer she received and that was the reason, her answer was ready on her fingertips.

The HR guy looked at her. They were used to meet people who were in their early twenties and who wanted to leave everything to achieve their dreams and they also knew ways of shattering those dreams to keep their company going. What do they call it? Ah! Retaining a valuable employee.

He said, "Tell me one thing – what's there for you in cooking? There's just space for Vikas Khanna and Sanjeev Kapoor. It will take you a lifetime to be at their place. And even if you win this World Food Festival, you wouldn't just replace them, right?"

Tiasha kept quiet as he continued, "...On the other hand, I have heard from Mohit that you have been doing extremely well in the advertising business. If you work like this, you could be in Mohit's position in two years. Why do you want to leave a..."

Had this been the Tiasha of two days back, she would have given in to this argument. But, today, she was clear and precise about what she wanted. She replied, "For the first time in my life, I am sure of something, and this won't change."

"Which means that you will have to breach the contract mid-way and resign," the HR guy said with a taut face. He looked rigid.

Tiasha said, "I would have never liked leaving things mid-way. But, if that's the only way out, I will..."

Just when she was about to complete her decision in a heated meeting room, Mohit intervened, "Can you work for six hours a day from Mahabaleshwar?"

There was pin-drop silence in the meeting room. Anushi looked at Mohit and from his expressions she knew that he wanted to retain her at any cost. Tiasha too, looked at Mohit pensively.

Thinking for less than a minute, she said, "Yes. Not really sure about the hours, but I will complete my tasks, if that's an option."

Mohit turned to Naina and said, "Naina, I feel let's give Tiasha this chance. For the first ten days, let's see if she can work from Mahabaleshwar. I was discussing this competition with her and I guess she can work at night. If she does well, we could let her continue. Else, resignation is always an option."

Tiasha loved it when Mohit backed her. She knew his experience was the sole factor on which he took such decisions and she knew he would have never taken them if she didn't work well. She felt valued for the first time in the meeting. Well, putting posters of 'You are valuable' never help. These little things make you feel valued. *Haina?*

With her eyes, she thanked him. He saw that, but chose not to respond. *He was a bit annoyed.*

The HR guy thought about it and responded, "Alright. Just because you guys are keen, I think we can work this out. All the best, Tiasha."

Mohit smiled and thanked the HR guy. Naina wished Tiasha good luck as they all vacated the meeting room. Just then, Mohit asked Tiasha to stay.

He said, "You know that I hardly bother about dreams and choices random kids make. But, your dream is a strange one. I don't know why, but I want to support it. And you know that this is perhaps the first and the last time that I would personally want to tell you that if you are risking so many things, work hard and achieve them. Win both games – office and your dream."

True, it was the first time when Mohit was not diplomatic; he was speaking from his heart, Tiasha felt. And assuring him, she said, "Trust me Mohit, I can and I definitely will stand up to your expectations. Your support meant a lot to me today."

On that note, Tiasha chose a margarita over a fully-loaded vegetable pizza and the best part was that she was like that little kid, who even after my comments still wanted to have the pizza. Perhaps, choices are like that – once you take them, just listen to your heart! *Like Aakaash said, she had created her choice today!*

Part - IV

The World Food Festival!

Dressed in a black skater dress, with minimum make-up and her hair tied in a systematic princess ponytail, Tiasha stood at the corner of a room full of dance, drinks and introductions.

She had reached Mahabaleshwar in the afternoon and as the tradition for the World Food Festival directed, the first event was the Prom. Shaped pretty socially, the idea behind the prom was to quickly mingle all the participants with each other and have some healthy interactions over drinks and food. The organisers, judges and participants had to spend a good one month together and therefore, the bonding was important, the organisers believed.

However, little did they know that people like Tiasha too existed in a world of social beings. Only she knew how much she missed Aakaash. It was only he, who could make these boring social gatherings entertaining. *Just like I would prefer having tea at Huda City Centre than being at such a party.*

Although Tiasha was extremely happy with the venue and the arrangements that were made, she missed her stand-up comedian. When she entered the resort with her luggage, everything looked dream-like. The rooms were allotted systematically, the resort was decorated with posters and hoardings and all one could feel round was food.

However, the idea of making new friends and dancing didn't really appeal to her. Out of all seventy participants, nobody really wanted to make friends or relationships, right? Everyone is here to win, spending a whooping twelve thousand on their registrations. Tiasha just found all of it fake. She picked up a mocktail and observed everyone from a distance.

While she looked around, for a minute, her eyes stopped at one person in the crowd, who stood exactly opposite to her, on the bar table, enjoying his beer.

Rajiv Tondon! Before coming to Mahabaleshwar, Tiasha had researched a lot about his work, his recipes, the kind of methods he used in cooking and similar information. She was a pro in stalking, I must acknowledge. However, as she looked at him, she felt the zeal to know more about him.

Sometimes, doesn't it happen...we want more of a person. At times, it's the mystery around them that pulls us towards them. It was exactly that what she felt about him!

♌

Dressed in a gray shirt with his sleeves folded up to his elbows, frameless spectacles suiting his dusky complexion, formal black chinos and a smile that would make anyone fall for him. His face had an unknown seriousness, perhaps a pretentious one, but it looked real.

Tiasha kept staring at him for a moment. Perhaps, if she would admit, she was really awe-struck by his personality. He looked much more handsome than he looked in his photographs.

The other factor, apart from his dapper looks and dressing choices, was his achievements. He was one of India's most renowned chefs at twenty-nine years of age; he had undergone a journey and was a self-made man. He achieved success because of his sheer individuality and Tiasha was always impressed by people who were individualistic. We know that by now, don't we?

So, as she looked at him and drooled over his persona for a minute, she realised she was the only one standing awkwardly in a corner and staring at strangers. *A judging point for everyone, for sure, eh?*

Therefore, making her way away from the dance floor and the smell of alcohol, she walked outside, towards the lobby. She asked at the reception, "Where can I get some cigarettes, madam?"

The receptionist looked at her, scanned her from top to toe and then replied, "Sorry ma'am, it's late and the tuck shop at the resort is closed. I can only help you out in the morning."

Tiasha smoked only when she was in two situations – one, when she was extremely stressed, and the other, when Aakaash wasn't around. With him revolving like the orbits around the sun, she would never get a chance to even look at her cigarettes.

However, being alone, she wanted to smoke, at least to get out of the party zone. How madly bored she was, only she knew. Have you ever observed, with some people, even a silent walk could be mesmerizing whereas, at times, even the loudest music is unable to keep you entertained. Tiasha was bored, even when she was amidst trillion of faces. All she needed was a break!

However, hill stations are smaller and calmer places. People generally retire to their houses at sunset.

Mahabaleshwar too was a town which beamed with silence and the beauty of nature, but when the sun bid adieu, it became uncomfortably silent. *It's happened with me as well that whenever I visited any hill station, the morning is beautiful, afternoons are sunny and the sunset makes everything dull.*

There was a silence in the atmosphere, which Tiasha felt was weird. Now, imagine someone from a noisy city like Gurgaon, where the horns and cars don't let you sleep, ends up in a place as silent as this.

Tiasha just faked a smile at the receptionist and walked towards the gate of the resort.

There, she asked the guard, "*Bhaiya, cigarette kidhar milega?*"

She was not able to digest the fact that she was alone, had no one whom she could trouble. The town was slightly taking over her mind with the silence all around.

Like the receptionist, the guard too scanned her and gave her that look which elders give you while saying, '*Baccha bigad gaya humara*'. He replied, half-heartedly, "There's a small shop around the corner."

Tiasha thanked him and as she started to look around, she could see narrow roads with steep turns, the cars sleeping peacefully in the parking slots, the guards of the resorts still yawning but awake and the city dampened with moist dew. It was almost midnight by then and the little town wanted to have a tranquil sleep, it seemed.

But, as Tiasha made her way till the little shop and while she was taking out money from her wallet, she asked the shopkeeper, "*Jaldi se ek packet Goldflake dena.*"

The next voice startled her.

"The tuck closes too early, *haina?*"

She looked up, startled, to find Rajiv there. With a smirk on his face that made him look hotter, he continued, smoking from the cigarette he had lit a while ago, "The loud music gets on my nerves too."

Tiasha freaked out for a moment. How could Rajiv be in front of her…for real (P.S.: Fan girl moment). She was almost about to behave abnormally, when she composed herself and lighting her cigarette, she replied, "Exactly. It's too much to take. And I get annoyed pretty easily."

Rajiv laughed. He looked all the more handsome when he did so. He asked, "Participant here?"

Tiasha nodded as she exhaled her smoke. While they chatted, the clouds seemed like they were catchable; they were so close to the beauty of nature. The serenity in the atmosphere might be unusual initially, but it grows on one. Even if for a second, Tiasha and Rajiv left their addiction aside and let themselves be, the moment could have been so beautiful. *Only if...*

Unfortunately, ignoring the nature-kissed beauty, they enjoyed each other's company as they walked back towards the resort. Tiasha asked, "You know you are the best mentor we'll have here, don't you?"

His attitude pretty much defined that he was aware of the fact very well. And without being modest, he replied, "Yes, I do. But, do you know one thing?"

Tiasha looked at him, as he continued, "No mentor can make a chef. These guys offered a good amount for me to be here for four weeks and I agreed, but otherwise, culinary art isn't something I can teach you or you can learn from me."

"Not just cooking makes a chef succesful. Confidence and zeal play a crucial role too. There, we'd need your help." This might sound flattering but the way Tiasha spoke didn't look like she was flattered. She was anyway being honest, which she generally was!

With an attitude that matched his, with flair in her voice competing with his and with extreme confidence in her eyes, she was someone who definitely impressed him. He replied, "Not a lot of people get to disagree with me."

He winked.

Tiasha was marked 'proud' immediately. As she bid him a good night, she walked towards her room and did not look back. She believed that those who are too used to attention should be handled normally; that makes things much more comfortable. She was a fan of his, she drooled over his looks, his personality, but to express it – *na na*, that wasn't Tiasha's cup of tea at all.

ᘓ

Fantasizing about a crush is something we've all done, and statistics prove...it's exciting.

As soon as Tiasha entered her room, she took out her phone, opened almost all possible social media apps and stalked Rajiv on all of them. She sent him a follow request on Instagram as she stalked through his pictures.

'He looks so damn hot, man!', she said to herself as she lay on her bed and scrolled through his pictures. As she saw each picture, she judged him by the caption and his expressions. Some pictures impressed her, while in the others, disappointment was all that she got.

'Too cheesy, this one is,' she sighed, looking at one of his pictures.

She scrolled down till the pictures posted a year ago. His eyes, she would say, were the most honest ones. However, by her analysis and research, she felt he was slightly pretentious and both cunning and manipulative.

And, mind you, she judged all of it only by looking at his pictures. Well, next level of being judgemental! And if that was less, here's more – she didn't press the like button for a single photograph. *Usse pata jo chal jaata that our Tiasha was stalking him!* Tiasha could write a book on stalking, and I am sure, her book would become a bestseller the day it would be launched!

She simply sent him an Instagram request. In a millisecond, Rajiv accepted her follow request, but did not follow her back. *Attitude ka problem number one. Ego toh bhadak gaya abb.* Tiasha was almost offended, but she knew the hierarchy between them, and hence, being practical, she forgave him for being ignorant. Her highness forgave him, *haan.*

He has quite a bit of arrogance in him, she registered as she slept, thinking about the new person she had just met.

Some encounters with people are like the taste of the ice candy that you have. Remember *kala khatta,* rose, mango and various flavours that a candy man adds to that ice candy? You are just unable to identify which flavour you endear the most.

The cake that they baked!

While Tiasha embarked on a new journey of food and beverages, Aakaash had hopped on a journey we typically called 'relationship'.

Too quick successions, you must be wondering. But, the way he was at that point of time, he needed someone he could confide in. His feelings were true, his love was real, but the person for whom they were intended was someone who ran away from these. Ironically, Aashna, who devotedly loved him was near him, yet far, and those who were far were still closer to his heart!

Still, he tried to be present where he was.

Aashna was very serious about him and so was he; he liked being pampered and cared for as well and she was the first person who actually helped him realise this. Ever since, he thought he knew himself, but when Aashna cared for him like no one else did, he felt treasured. His days would start with her at breakfast, lunch would be with her and dinner too would be in her vicinity.

He was enjoying her company and she was feeling adored by his care. Aakaash never thought Tiasha acknowledged his concern as much as Aashna did. She was happy because he cared for her and she cared for him because she really was concerned. *Too much caring, haan?*

And, between this sugar-coated caring and *coochy coo,* Aakaash made sure he didn't forget his best friend. Whenever she called, he would take her call; whenever she texted, he would reply – just that the zeal with which he typed those messages was slightly decreasing. Now, that zeal was towards Aashna.

However, Tiasha was still an inevitable part of his routine. She would still be his priority and he would still check her message before anyone else's. Some positions in life are just reserved for some people; no matter how far they go, that place stays theirs.

On the other hand, Tiasha was loving where she was; she had finally created her choice, as her best friend called it.

You know, a few months back, there was some construction going around my workplace and we had to walk till the office gates. That's great, right? But, let me tell you something secretive. Every morning, when I walked towards the office, the path that I took was walked upon. After all, everyone walked on that path to reach office. I didn't bother looking at any other alternative at that time.

This is strange, because I never took the path everybody was walking on. Hamesha, I felt ki apna rasta khud banao...we can do that for ourselves, at least. But, at that time, I was doing what everyone else was, which is good, trust me. There's no problem with it, just that I knew I was doing something someone else could do as well.

Similarly, one day I was drafting a mail to the client and while following the standard template, I realised that it was easy for me to cut someone else's name and paste mine there. That dispensible we all were. And, to learn, that's okay. But, once the zeal of taking that road not taken starts building inside your head, aur kuch nahi dikhta fir, howsoever lovely it might be.

Tiasha's case was similar. In fact, she was walking on the third road, which was her own. She had created an option and was walking upon that! Perhaps, the two of them were baking their own cakes. One was happily decorating his cake with cherries and almonds of love and care. The other was adding much more delight to her chocolate cake by being ambitious. They were both working equally hard on their careers but were just in two different recipe books as of now – one with a new partner in life and the other, fantasising about an absolutely handsome mentor.

In a way, both of them were finding escapes from each other. Don't you think so? I should actually call them *Immature Fits*!

That orange candy!

If you haven't tried, there's one thing I suggest you should. Every day, when you get up in the morning, just walk up towards a window or a balcony. Close your eyes and feel the atmosphere around you. Even if there's nothing extremely luscious or green, just feel the morning.

I do that regularly and feeling the morning sensitizes each cell in the body to work harder. While the first edits of our book were going on, we lost the edits, which meant reworking on almost twenty thousand words in a timeline which I was already struggling to meet. Now, the day I realised that my edits went missing, trust me, I took the whole world on my head. I got so irritated that I just behaved abnormally – calling Mom and Dad from the Metro and crying, cribbing endlessly to my sister, calling our publisher at midnight and sleeping with a hassled mind. I wasn't upset because *mehnat karni padti, wo mujhe pata hai main kar leti.* The reason I was heart-broken was that I had really poured out the purest emotions and losing out on those emotions in form of words would have shattered me.

Next morning, I got up with a terrible headache, as if I had gulped litres of beer the previous night, but there was one thing which wasn't as troublesome. As I walked towards my balcony, which I devotedly do every day, I stood with my arms open and felt the morning. The sun was orangish and was smiling brightly at me, the breeze was calm – the one which we have when winter is about to begin – and the ambience of the morning was blossoming with positivity. And amidst this, just one message that Anisha wrote to me the previous night blinked in my mind,

'Agar ho bhi gaye kharab edits, toh book toh tum likhogi hi na. Aise hi toh nahi de dogi.'

And what dad said, 'This time, we'll have a better edit. And when you did the edits, I am sure you can do them again. So, stop cribbing and start working Devu!'

Exactly, stop cribbing and start working, Devu, I told myself and with the thought that the edits would now be a notch higher, your author started the day! Part of the routine, I sat in the Metro and started editing from page 1, when I just thought to scan all my devices as I have a habit of keeping multiple back-ups, and luckily, we found one! *Thoda sa rework hua, but at least the emotions which were close to the heart stayed there.*

Mornings bring positivity and like the sun shines every day, without complaining of the clouds hindering its way, don't you think we can go on without cribbing as well? *Sabse pehle toh main ye implement kar lun!*

But, on a serious note, mornings are magical. Your brain too is free of the complications, after all!

♌

For Tiasha too, every morning in Mahabaleshwar was blissful. Actually, every morning becomes blissful when you work for yourself, after all.

As Tiasha got up and looked outside her window, she felt delighted to see such a clear sky. As much as she disliked the mountains in the evening, she loved the place during dawn. She opened the huge glass window and let the breeze brush her face. Standing there and looking at the scenic beauty of the hills, Tiasha thought about Aakaash.

As much as she tried to be cool with Aashna being in Aakaash's life, she was affected. She didn't want any expectations from the person she was with, but at the same time, she silently expected Aakaash to always be near her. Strange are our expectations from those whom we love. You know, I've noticed, our worst mood swings are always with the people we are closest to!

At times, I knew I was being irrational and dumb, but I would still fight and argue.Those who are around, even with the worst mood swings, are those who you know will never let you get lost. We can crib only in front of those who wouldn't judge you for cribbing and you can shout only at those who you know would not leave you even after seeing the worst of you! Jo sabse closest hote hai, wo hi sabse zyada sunte hai! Haina?

That was exactly Tiasha's case. And just while she was thinking so, her phone buzzed.

It was a notification for the first session with Rajiv today. The food festival organisers had divided the participants into groups of fifteen. And Tiasha, being in the first batch had her session with Rajiv and then with Nishima, the second judge and mentor.

She quickly took a shower, got into her formal trousers and a high neck pink formal shirt, quickly added a brush of gloss to her lips and picking up her cell phone, rushed towards the conference room.

♌

"Why do you think you dream to become a chef?"

Rajiv asked arrogantly to a forty-five year old lady, who he was in a conversation with. He had some seriously impressive oration skills, Tiasha added to her 'Stalking Rajiv' list. But, he had some extremely sharp arrogance skills as well.

I really wonder if he ever visited any school where they taught manners, Tiasha registered and added this as well to that list. She was absolutely annoyed with people who didn't know how to be courteous. Impulsively, she raised her voice as she said, "I don't think dreams need a reason to be dreamt, sir."

Every chef in the house looked at her. From amateur to seasoned chefs, everyone just gave her blank expressions. However, she stood with her head high. Whenever she took a stand, she stood firm on that stand.

She continued, "We dream because the dream is to achieve what we have dreamt of. I am sorry but you can't ask for reasons to dream. The dream in itself is the reason."

Rajiv looked at her, calculated her confidence and was extremely impressed by her determination. It was as if he saw himself in the mirror when he looked at her. However, disguising the respect that he had for her determined approach, just to prove that he was the boss in the room, he snapped, "No matter how correct and brilliant the answer was, was the question directed towards you, Miss Tiasha Shah?"

Tiasha replied, as firmly and egoistically she could, "No."

"Then, I suggest please do not answer till you are asked to," he said looking straight into her eyes. Anger was evidently visible in his eyes too. And her eyes expressed anxiety as well. She knew he was the star chef in the room and not her, she knew he was correct and she knew she was too intrusive into everyone's life at times. Noting all these points, Tiasha suppressed her anger and sat down. But, Rajiv was marked minus hundred in humility immediately in her stalking list.

Throughout the next two hours, when Rajiv spoke, Tiasha didn't utter a word. It always happened to her – if she felt bad, either she would explosively bomb the area, or she would burst a volcano inside her and keep quiet. And trust me, when she kept quiet, her expressions and her wide eyes spoke tales about her being upset.

Rajiv definitely noted her expressions and calculated her anger, and yet again, he could find traces of himself in her.

♌

Later during lunch, while Tiasha sat and lunched with some seasoned chefs from around the country, her phone buzzed with an Instagram notification.

Rajiv had sent her a follow request.

'Interesting, isn't it? First, pretend to have ignored to follow someone, then insult the same person in front of her colleagues and then send a follow request to cover that up. Go to hell, Rajiv Tondon. I don't think I should respond to your request.' Tiasha spoke to herself.

She happily ignored the notification and kept her phone aside. However, one thing which she thought later, with a peaceful mind was that Rajiv wasn't wrong either. In fact, for some strange reason, she found his personality magnetic.

She could easily see through his arrogance and his 'star-like' behaviour. No, there was no layer to it, but still Tiasha had started to admire him because it's only admiration that leads to you getting affected so much by someone. She was getting inclined towards his personality and the way he handled himself.

Even while having her lunch, she didn't miss stealing a glance at him. In a purple shirt, he looked extremely decent and formal. His smile was as always captivating and his ruffled hair made him look all the more cute. For a second, Tiasha couldn't decide whether he was more cute or more hot and therefore, she preferred believing he was more arrogant and hence, easy to ignore.

As I said, like the two flavours in the candy, it was still getting tough for her to judge if he was annoying and flamboyant or just a star who had a 'star-like' personality. For a minute, she wanted to sway close to him and the next minute, she wanted to sway away from him.

Perhaps, it was also a repel effect of Aakaash's relationship.

Just like the sweet-sour flavour of the orange candy we used to love during our childhood. Remember the orange round-shaped toffee? My mom used to love it and so did I!

Exactly like that, Tiasha was too confused to understand what the flavour was of the new person she had let in to her thoughts! Arrogant and sweet at the same time, manipulative and honest at the same instance – this man was mysterious, she thought!

♌

After having another session with Nishima Kapoor, Tiasha quickly rushed to her room. It was already 7:30 p.m. by then. Remember, she also had her duties towards Apticon which she had to fulfil? Quickly getting into her loose t-shirt and a pair of cotton shorts, Tiasha started checking her mails. She dropped a message to Anushi and Mohit, writing,

Started working. The assigned tasks would be done by 3:30 a.m.

Anushi replied immediately, *I am sure, it will be. Take care. Good night.*

Mohit sent a thumbs up emoji and Tiasha started working on an advert that she had to create for her brand. Mohit had mentioned that it had to be a notch higher, typical of his advice at the beginning of each project. However, Tiasha really respected Mohit. He might have been strict or rude at times, but after working with him for quite some time, she knew that being assertive too was essential. As Mohit generally said, 'In corporate, trust people but trust them with a rationale.' Tiasha had a reason to trust him for she saw his work to be nearly perfect. Silently, she admired people who admired their work. And hence, she really wanted to do a great job.

Ignoring the tiredness and exhaustion, she quickly started to focus.

At nine, her phone buzzed with a notification for dinner. *Fancy stuff, these guys had planned, I must say.*

Every night, there was a lavish dinner which was served for all the participants, but as Tiasha was working, she called for a simple dinner in her room itself. Looking at Tiasha grow from the interview day till today makes me feel happy for her. What about you?

As the clock tickled from eight to ten and ten to twelve, Tiasha kept brainstorming for ideas and kept working diligently on her laptop. She was extremely tired and in desperate need of sleep, but she had to stay firm on her word and therefore, ignoring the signs of tiredness her body gave, she just got up and walked downstairs to get a smoke.

I wonder at times, how easy it is for people like Tiasha, (who will hate me for sure when I say so) who can easily de-stress by having a cigarette or two? Judgmental much? PS: I'd say this is the standard statement of a non-smoker, haina?

Anyways...she walked till the little shop she purchased cigarettes from the previous night, to find Rajiv there, once again. Tiasha gave him a blank look. Remember their morning encounter? Yes. That.

He looked at her and smiled, knowing pretty well that she would be offended by the way he had spoken to her in front of everyone. He knew Tiasha was egoistic and being of a similar sort, he expected a similar reaction from her. He smiled at the fact that she had guessed her reaction correctly!

Tiasha lit her cigarette and after taking a smoke or two, started walking towards the resort with the cigarette in her hand. Rajiv didn't say anything but just walked beside her. He said, "Personal and professional are two different arenas, Tiasha. I respect you personally doesn't necessarily mean that I will be nice to you professionally too. I know you felt bad in the morning, but technically, I don't owe you any explanation."

Tiasha heard him carefully and while listening to him, her brisk walk became slower. He apparently made a lot of sense. She replied, "That's true, Rajiv. In fact, I am sorry as well for the blunt replies. Too habitual of being over-confident."

He laughed. Tiasha was flattered by his looks.

"I was pretty much the same, hence I relate to you."

Silence prevailed for a while, after which Rajiv asked, "You didn't come for dinner?"

Tiasha was flattered by the fact that he noticed that she wasn't present. She was overwhelmed, but hiding the awe-struck expression, she replied subtly, "Yes, I am working for my office from here. So till three or four, I'll work. Hence, after the mandatory sessions, I am off to my room except for this short break."

"Why?" he quipped.

"Because I don't like quitting things mid-way."

"You are extremely stubborn, aren't you?" he commented. She was a workaholic, just like he was. If I am allowed to make the cliché comment, *mujhe toh ye rab ne bana di jodi hi lagti hai!*

Tiasha smiled and while sorting some professional differences, they reached the resort. As Tiasha threw the cigarette away, Rajiv asked, "Also, I sent you a follow request, which you haven't accepted yet. Now that you don't hate me as much as you did in the afternoon, you might consider accepting it."

Tiasha replied with a wink, "You took a day to send a request; let me take another day to respond to it."

Saying so, she retired to her room and worked till late in the night. After mailing the first drafts to Mohit and Anushi, she hardly was left with three hours to sleep. She just crashed on the bed and slept till the alarm rang the next morning, starting the same routine again.

Conversational!

The routine in Mahabaleshwar was pretty exciting and interesting for Tiasha. Even when it was exhaustive, what would be better than being among people who breathed spices and lived cooking?

You know, I am an extremely bad chef since forever. Given a chance to be in the kitchen alone, I can be sure of ruining each possible ingredient inside it. That's the sole reason I don't even enter the kitchen. And that's also the reason I love chefs so much. Anyone can win my heart by making me the best food! To cook and to love to cook are two different things, after all!

For Tiasha, being in a space where she interacted with so many participants, spoke to them about their journeys and shared her ideas and recipes was more than sufficient to be happy. And adding to all of that was her friendship with Rajiv which kept her engaged.

Every midnight, their walk had become a schedule. Considering their highly lit egos, their arguments too were becoming a routine. They had similar perspectives, but even if they differed a bit, none of them would take a step back.

While I write of differences, I just realised something. Aakaash and Tiasha were two opposite zodiacs – Sagittarius and Cancer, respectively. While Sagis are expected to be indifferent, Cancerians are affected by the smallest things. Emotions too, while Sagis are silent sufferers, a Cancerian would move the world if they were hurt. Complete opposites they were, yet, whenever they were together, the differences didn't seem important. Only togetherness did. One, they never were short of conversations, because if not anything, they could always argue and crib. Two, even if they ever had differences, for both of them, the other person mattered more than winning an argument. For Aakaash, to be with her was more important than winning an argument. Here, with Rajiv, each argument had repel effects. You know, ego, sadism, etc. That was the difference!

But, one thing that impressed Rajiv the most was Tiasha's sense of experimentation and her risk-taking skills! She was someone who would take risks despite of the fact that each dish was being evaluated; one wrong experiment and things could go haywire. Yet, she took those risks!

From beetroot cake to peanut burfi cooked in olive oil, from *arbi ki kadhi* to *aamrakhand* – Rajiv was genuinely mesmerised by her style of cooking. In fact, the way she cooked and the way she handled herself surprised him. *He thought she was a stubborn kid, after all.* Not even a single drop of extra oil would you find in her vegetables and not even a grain she would waste. That was perhaps the true definition of a good cook, he believed.

Almost halfway through the World Food Festival, Tiasha had spent almost two weeks sleeping less than four hours and working like an insomniac. Slowly, but evidently, the threads that linked her to the ground were slipping off from her hands. Remember when I said, as she took the leap, Aakaash bid her adieu from the ground. Perhaps, she was so busy flying high that the ground looked too far from her zenith.

It was extremely strange that even when Aakaash and Tiasha were connected like buddies till a week before, they were now almost like the forgotten friends because Aakaash was busy in his relationship and stand-up and Tiasha felt like an intruder in his life when they spoke now. They didn't have a lot to speak about, except the Food Festival. Hence, while they got attracted to two different set of people, their bond with each other started falling weak, or at least that's what they thought!

Now, she was in her world, and he in his.

It was visible through Tiasha's face that she was tired and Rajiv admired her dedication to work. She worked insanely. He felt that before the knock-out round begun, Tiasha needed a day's break from her extremely hectic routine. Therefore, that night when they were walking, Rajiv asked, "Mahabaleshwar is beautiful and they have some great farm fresh fruits. You know it's the hub of jams and fruit juices, right?"

Tiasha smiled and replied, looking up at the clouds she always wanted to catch hold of, "Yes, I know that. You are interested in the history of Mahabaleshwar is something I don't know though."

Tiasha laughed. He was the judge of the competition she was a participant of, they had some serious ego issues while working, but somehow, there was comfort when both of them spoke to each other. Maybe being egoistically similar had built that for them.

Also, let's not forget, there were ideologies they shared which were similar, there were emotions they thought they didn't feel, and there was work, which both of them worshipped. They *had* to like each other's company; they were perfectly similar in a few ways, haina?

Anyway, calculating her extremely funny expressions, Rajiv gave up and said, "Madam, will you come out with me for lunch tomorrow?"

Tiasha smiled and gave him the 'I knew it all' expression. She laughed out loud, "That I will for sure, Rajiv. But, Mahabaleshwar is beautiful...too cliché. Too much Bollywood, eh?"

Rajiv smiled sheepishly; it was so evident that he was extremely awkward. His forte was in arguing and being arrogantly rude. Being sweet...*thoda mushkil tha yaar!*

He replied, "You know, you are a notorious little kid."

Attraction or infatuation – there was something which was trying to seep in between the formal friendship. Maybe, or maybe not! *Kabhi kabhi,* non-opposites attract. These two were perfect for each other, no?

What she was looking for in Aakaash was here in Rajiv. He was exactly like her – a person who would always let go of expectations, he wasn't someone who'd wait for you till midnight for dinner; he wasn't someone who would caringly bring you chocolates to woo you. He was rather someone extremely frank and blunt. Sorry was one word he would say only if he meant it. What took to nurture a relationship, both of them didn't know. Ironically, Tiasha was happier with him around because she was free from those expectations.

That was exactly what Tiasha wanted from someone in her life, right? But then, why did she miss a spark which existed earlier in her life, I wonder.

Actually, if you remember, when Aakaash found his perfect match, his approach too was similar; these two were insane little kids, trust me!

Love is complicated, as I always say. Meri baat maano hi mat.

♌

The next afternoon was conversational.

Tiasha and Rajiv went out for lunch and had a sumptuous lunch in an open restaurant, amidst strawberry farms. *Oh God! This sounds like one of the old British Romantic Poetry! I know, I know!*

"Have you been in love?" Tiasha asked casually, breaking the ice which Rajiv always formed around his personal life. He was quite mysterious.

Rajiv chewed the salad he was eating and replied, "Yes. But, *had.*"

Whenever love, as a word, is used in past tense, there are trillions of stories that jump out of the eyes. Break-up, the solitude, the loneliness...but not even one of them were visible in Rajiv's eyes. He was not casual about love, this Tiasha knew, but nor was she able to see any seriousness that he had for love.

On the one hand, Tiasha didn't want a burden of a relationship, but when someone else took the feeling lightly, she was judging him. *Kitni buddhu hai ye ladki!*

Looking at Tiasha's expressions, Rajiv continued, "What's your story? Not really in love?"

Tiasha snapped, "I asked the question first."

"I answered your question. Wrong question to choose. Now, you answer my question." He smirked.

While they chatted amidst red and luscious strawberries looking beautiful, Tiasha ordered for fresh cream with strawberries, which was one dish she had heard everyone talk about. The strawberries were cut and served with fresh cream. *The fresh cream is as fresh as the strawberries and the taste of the juicy red strawberries...Oh! That was just out of this world.*

So, while tasting it, Tiasha thoughtfully replied, "I wouldn't say I was in love. I would say, I am still in love with my best friend. But, like a best friend. Things could not work out when love seeped in. But, that doesn't mean we were at odds with each other!"

I didn't expect this answer. Neither did you, right? (Honestly, Tiasha *ne khud bhi nahi socha hoga.*)

No one spoke for a while. An awkward silence prevailed.

"You know what, *when things don't work, you do,*" Rajiv said.

The only thing that made her grow fond of him was his workaholic behaviour. When he prioritized his passion over everything, Tiasha felt inspired. She knew he could leave everything aside to work. Proving this fact, he added, "I like being truthful and hence, since always, I told my girl that whenever there would be a choice of choosing between her and my dream, I'll always choose my dream over her. That was always a given. I always thought I was practical and logical, but I couldn't get away with the melodrama after break-up. I got affected, affected my work and then went into depression... all that drama! Since then, my funda is to stay far away from commitment.

He sighed. Tiasha looked at him and without filtering what she was thinking, she bloated out, "Frankly, Rajiv, it doesn't seem like you were affected by the way you are talking."

Ah-ah! You go and tell someone that *bro, it doesn't feel like you are hurt when the person is upfront accepting how affected he was. Not a great move, Tiasha.*

However, being Rajiv, he was subtle. He replied, "The recipes that you know me for made me what I am and not my relationship. Why should I let the sorrow of one path I have left behind take over the happiness that I have created for myself on another path?"

"Bang on!" Tiasha exclaimed.

If he saw himself in her, she saw her ideologies in him. And like the fresh cream and strawberry dessert, she felt Rajiv's company was easy going and enjoyable. But, at the same time, like after having a sweet, our heart craves for something salted, even Tiasha knew that one part of her heart still resided in the Delhi apartment next to hers.

While she said it didn't matter, her heart knew how every selfie that Aashna and Aakaash posted pinched her. The fact that she would have to permanently let go of her best friend troubled her – but, ego, o ego! She didn't express anything to him. Rather, she pretended as if she was the happiest, when she very well knew she wasn't.

You know that feeling...that someone you have a crush on gets engaged to someone else, is really scary. Imagine, one morning you get up to find out that the love of your life, someone you rely on, has decided to get married to someone else because, well, he wants to. Imagine how would it feel? There would be sensations and emotions you wouldn't even recognise but effect toh hoga! Haina?

Bas, wahi effect tha Tiasha par.

Didn't I tell you…nahi aaega samajh. Complicated stuff!

Perfects are perfects together'?'

It's said that time flows when you are happy and it starts to move sluggishly when you are not. Every time, at the brink of a journey, everyone seems to be extremely excited about that journey to begin, but going forward, slowly, the spark of the excitement starts reducing and reality starts becoming evident.

When Tiasha left for Mahabaleshwar twenty-five days ago, Aakaash had taken a decision to leave the strings that bonded him with her and let himself get one more chance to fall in love and feel love. (Though this sounds melodramatic and too Bollywood-ish, this is how the situation was. Bear with it, please.)

Aakaash had accepted the fact that Tiasha and his relation didn't work because of their ideological differences and as per his understanding, being with someone who has similar expectations from a relationship would simplify his life.

However abrupt it might sound, I am going to narrate to you my next statement.

Aakaash felt exactly how Tiasha felt – suffocated in the web of care and love. When someone is not used to care and all of a sudden gets pampered, they might happily accept it for a while, but till when? After a point of time, everything becomes a little stifling.

On a personal note, I feel it's about perspectives. We might want to judge Aakaash for being mean to a girl as sweet as Aashna, but if he felt suffocated, he did. It wasn't as if he had deliberately planned that he'll feel suffocated after a month, right? And secondly, relationships are transient; love is what goes on forever. While Aakaash was happily surviving a relationship with Aashna, love perhaps was there in Mahabaleshwar.

"You had your job interview today, didn't you?" Aakaash asked in an angry tone.

"I left it. Your birthday was much more special than the interview, Aakaash," she replied holding on to his elbow.

Aakaash nodded his head in disappointment and frowned angrily.

"Would you expect me to leave a stand-up session to give you a birthday surprise, Aashna?" he asked as they walked past Vigyan Bhawan, between the molecules of lights lighting the ambience. Delhi is chaotic and full of traffic jams, but there are some places here which are serene – one of them being the road that walked parallel to the Vigyan Bhawan. The roads were lit with the lights that looked like molecules and the best part was that it just lit the whole atmosphere. The darkness was scared off by the brightness of truth!

Amidst those bright roads, Aashna walked with Aakaash, hand in hand.

She was dressed beautifully in a pink lace dress, *just for him.* She wanted to make his day special. Little did he know, he couldn't take a lot of attention; he was habitual of giving that attention and never receiving it.

Aashna replied, "I wouldn't expect it, but you would do that for me, wouldn't you? We don't force things when we love, Aakaash. But, we go out of our way to make the other person feel loved."

As Aakaash looked angrily at her petite face, he remembered how his friendship had been with Tiasha – they loved each other, but the idiots that they were, both of them refused to accept this fact!

Looking at Aashna, Aakaash knew it wasn't her fault as well. It was he who wasn't sure about anything when he had decided to be with her. Aashna was the same since he met him, it was just that today, he was analysing and critiquing the differences while in the beginning, he loved to observe the similarities. She had always kept him above all her priorities and worshipped their relationship the most. She was someone who nurtured their relationship like a baby – putting in all the care, the love and the emotions.

When he was with Tiasha, he did what Aashna was doing for him today. And he, at one point of time, was expecting someone to prioritize him over everything in their life. But, did he still think so was the question.

He always felt that he wanted to settle in a relationship and for that, having a perfect partner would definitely be the perfect thing in life.

He silently walked with her, without saying much. But, when his eyes looked at Aashna, he felt disgusted with himself for a second. A rush of guilt went through his spine and he immediately held her hand and gave her a tight hug. He felt he was the villain of this story and being Aakaash, he would drown with guilt if this was the case.

He said, as he took her face in the cup of his hands, "I know you'll hate me for what I say next, but, keeping you in the dark would be worse. Aashna—"

"No, I don't want to listen to anything!" was all that she said. Perhaps, knowing what was coming her way and perhaps being unprepared to accept it. Perhaps, being in denial.

She looked away when Aakaash brought her gaze towards his, once again. He knew he would have never wanted to be in that position, but he was. He said, looking straight in her eyes, "You know, even if I stay here, I will never be able to stay here. And when my mind is not around, how will I be loyal to you? Wouldn't that be worse?"

Aashna looked dejected. She had fat tears rolling down her eyes. She had a sensitive heart which was silently being butchered into small pieces. Imagine her situation – a fan girl, who had written to her favourite comedian on YouTube, managed to get his number and proposed to him, who she had fantasized about. She hadn't just lived with him for a month – she had lived with his videos for more than six months and even after giving so much and pampering that relationship – in fact, worshipping it, she still couldn't stop it from ending. It was flowing like sand from her hands and even if she tried to close her fist, she knew she wouldn't be able to save it.

Just like her tears, she knew she couldn't stop Aakaash. She knew he was way beyond attachment and emotions because his emotions towards Tiasha were triple-fold. Aashna said, "You know that Tiasha will not come back, right?"

"Yes," he replied.

"Yet?" she asked, perhaps trying to save her relationship for the last time. She really was dependent on him for her happiness, she believed.

"Yes, because I respect you and our bond, Aashna. Realising that the only person I can think about is Tiasha, how can I keep you in the dark? You don't deserve being cheated on," he replied, still walking with her, but in reality, walking away from her.

"If you wish, I will stay. And when we are together, I promise you that Tiasha will never come between the two of us. As I said, I don't want to demean the feelings both of us have for each other. You tell me Aashna. If you say, I'll stay here forever and you know, when I say forever, it will mean forever."

Aashna didn't say anything but gave him a hug and left... towards the darkness, or perhaps the lights that she wanted to find.

She knew Aakaash meant what he said. He would stay with her if she asked him to. But, can love be asked for? Can love be requested?

She knew that she wouldn't be able to detach him from the ambitious girl that Tiasha was. Perhaps, each person who comes in our life becomes an epitome of learning. *Kabhi notice karna,* you might feel bad and dejected with some people, but at the end, it all becomes one word – learning! Whether the relationship works or not, the learning always does!

Perhaps, Aakaash was not that eternal love that she had thought him to be, but a lesson of learning for Aashna, who could push her to be what she always wanted to be. His little cameo in her life perhaps changed her way of looking at life. *Nahi?*

On the other hand, you know what the best part about love is? It can neither be caught, nor set free. When you love someone, you will never be able to let go of them. But, when you don't, it wouldn't let you stay together.

Rose cucumber pasta – yes, it exists!

Nearing the end of the month-long competition, everyone was preparing and praying for their victory. They had spent a whole month in Mahabaleshwar and had spent ages waiting to be recognised. The day was nearing and the zeal in the air was becoming competitive. With just three days left for the World Food Festival to end, every finalist was on their toes.

The competition consisted of three rounds, first of which was where Tiasha was at the moment, preparing food without fire. Out of the final twelve, six would go ahead from here. And then, the second and third rounds would be on the last day of the festival. It was like the climax was built in a way that everyone would wait for a nail-biting finish.

Tiasha cooked well and everyone, including Rajiv knew this. While Tiasha was cooking dishes, there was one person who loved cooking up new stories...one who had landed in Mumbai this evening to travel to Mahabaleshwar.

I am not even gonna ask, 'Guesses?' like they ask in awards. It's so pretty obvious and my readers are smart enough to guess anyway!

Aakaash, who by the way, had signed a contract with a leading YouTube blogger to be a guest on his channel to narrate his first love story.

A comedian narrating a love story was phenomenally funny, *haina?*

Anyway, his flight of thoughts veered towards Mahabaleshwar, leaving all the emotional baggage behind.

♌

After the first round, when Tiasha stood with her dish in front of Rajiv and Nimisha, she blazed with happiness and confidence. She always knew when her dish was good and when it was, her eyes sparkled with confidence. She had prepared pasta without using any cheese or butter.

Rather, she used rose essence and cucumber to give her pasta an altogether different taste.

Sounds weird? Well, experiments are supposed to be so. But, those who experiment, innovate!

Rajiv said, as he took a spoon of the dish that she had prepared, "Interesting. I never knew pasta could be Indianised."

Tiasha replied, "When I was a kid, I loved when my granny would put cucumber and sugar in the *prasad* for Ganesh ji's *aarti*. When you gave us this challenge of cooking without fire, I could think of nothing but this. And then, rose became an improvisation."

Nimisha laughed, saying, "Seeing your panic attack at the start, I almost thought you'd end up messing everything up, Tiasha."

Everyone heard their conversation. Rajiv, however, intervened and said, "Of course not. She's a stubborn kid, ma'am. She can fight back in any situation."

Rajiv had built a soft corner for her when she had walked him out of her life. She genuinely didn't want an arrogant partner who could leave her in between the way called life. She had been longing for this space, but when she had an option of choosing that space for herself, she chose to choose her best friend. She respected Rajiv, but she loved Aakaash, she knew.

While looking at Rajiv as he announced the winners who went to the second round, Tiasha silently prayed to god to have Aakaash for herself.

P.S.: It's in situations as weird as this that your heart has to pump all the emotions.

"*God ji, yaar...I know I am confused and you must be thinking I should ask you to help me win, but I wanted something else. I know I am puzzled always, I know I get attracted to people like Rajiv...but at the end, I can't stay without my buddy, my best friend. I know Aakaash is an idiot, he scold me incessantly, gets dumb when he doesn't want to talk, gets quiet for no good reason, hurts my ego at times, keeps pestering me with his 'dos and don'ts' but with him, seven hours of being quiet can also be cherished. I don't know how strange it might sound to you, but perhaps he's the only person who I let scold me, who I let question my ego and who I let into my life. It is my choice to give him that right.*

He is stupid and dumb, but he knows what his Tiasha wants. With him, World Food Festival looks achievable. I just feel my feet are grounded and my wings are flying when he is around. Final decision, lock kar dijiye that I want my best friend for a lifetime. "

Smart wishes *haan*? She wanted Aakaash, but not a relationship. She loved his company, but would not want to stay with him. She loved him, but would not want to love the feeling called love. Oh god! How terribly confused this girl was!

But, wasn't she just like you and I, who are equally confused and stuck in between ways? I have been cribbing about Tiasha being confused throughout, but haven't you been in such situations at some point of time in life? Perhaps, she was just a reflection of what we were! Perhaps—

She was just like her dish – innovative yet conventional!

Who wins?

"All the best Tiyu. You know you have it in you to win it." Tiasha had reached the last round of the cooking competition and standing just a step away from a huge jump, she would never wear her apron without talking to her parents.

You know, personally, every time I sent the manuscript for edit, I called Maa and Papa too. Tiasha, I know how elated you feel before the last round, girl! I can relate to it completely.

Tiasha's parents were as happy as she was. They wholeheartedly wished her. After all, it was only them who stood by her throughout this month, when Aakaash was busy finding his happiness in his love and she was in dire need of inspiration to cook and be social throughout the day and work over the monotonous advertising projects at night. You need inspiration for that, bro.

Her parents were a constant support for her. They were always there, they are always there, and they would always be near her, today and forever, she knew.

On the other hand, she also looked at her phone, before switching the video call with her parents. She wouldn't accept, but she wanted Aakaash to call her and wish her for the day too.

Looking at the blank notification panel of her cell phone, she felt disappointed.

Little did she know that Aakaash was just a few steps away from her. He just stood outside her room, waiting for her to walk out to go to the competition and give her a surprise. Even when he knew her inside out, he wasn't too sure of how she would react to his arrival.

Love was funny, just like him, and love was serious, just like her!

After giving hugs and kisses to her parents over the call, she got up and was just brushing her hair before she left the room for the competition, when her eyes stopped at the chewing gum that was peeping out from her backpack.

It was the same backpack which she had given to Aakaash and she was sure he forgot to clear it out before returning it to her. That watermelon flavoured Orbit took the trail of her thoughts to just another world.

♌

"Trust me Aakaash, I'll throw you out of my room if you chew a chewing gum in front of me." She said authoritatively. But, more than authority, it was her pleading that was coated with a layer of authority.

Tiasha was funny. She got a strange feeling looking at someone chewing gum. She received weird sounds from her stomach and felt ticklish. She behaved hilariously when someone did so. And Aakaash loved to see her cute expressions. Hence, he made sure he always took out a chewing gum to trouble her.

Every time they would be together, Aakaash would take out his favourite chewing gum and would tease her. That was his favourite way of ticking her nerves and seeing her adorably admirable expressions.

And Tiasha, like a little kid, would just make weird faces and their fight would go on for a lifetime. At times, it was difficult to guess if they loved their fights or they fought through their love.

ᘚ

Those memories ran amok in her mind while she looked at the chewing gum. For once, Tiasha just laughed out loud at the crazy memories they created whenever they were together. She was smiling broadly as she applied the gloss on her lips. She got ready wearing a cotton khadi one piece as she dazzled with confidence.

As she saw herself smiling, how she really wished Aakaash would have been there. By the way, she still didn't know about Aashna and Aakaash's break-up. I am sure, a bhangra jig would have followed if she came to know about this. How she had prayed that the buddy she cherished would be exclusively hers. She really wanted to give him a tight hug and tell him that howsoever stupid he was, he was still all hers.

And just when Madam Tiasha was busy in fantasizing about Aakaash and herself, her phone buzzed.

Looking at the screen, her eyes were startled.

It was James, the chief editor of the magazine which sponsored the World Food Festival. Well, I just forgot to mention, James had flown from New York to select the best chef today. He had just reached the resort, but being the workaholic that he was, he didn't want to waste even a second. He had plans in his mind.

Tiasha did not expect a call from him, obviously. She believed he didn't even know about her existence. Tiasha took a minute to brace herself to talk to one of the leading icons in the industry, however, James did not even let her speak. As soon as she picked up the phone, he said, "Hey, could we meet in my room for ten minutes before your competition begins?"

With no second thoughts in her mind, Tiasha replied, "Of course, James. I'll see you in two minutes."

"Great! See you, Tiasha."

It was fun hearing him pronounce Tiasha's name. Tiasha too smiled at his accent as she quickly locked her room and was about to run, just to find someone standing there…chewing chewing-gum.

Tiasha was on cloud nine. It was as if all her fantasies had been approved. She wanted to just jump and give him a tight hug. For once she thought she was hallucinating about his presence; she wanted to run and give the idiot she was seeing a slap and then a tight hug again and she didn't want to leave him even for a second. But, just when the trail of her lovely thoughts started, she remembered that she had a meeting.

As Aakaash took a step ahead, Tiasha said, running towards James's room,

"I love you too. I just have a meeting. I'll be back and continue the rest."

Ahan! 'I-love-you-too'? The most confused person in the whole world had finally decided on what she really wanted in life? Or perhaps, just for that second, she was that happy and hence had explicitly expressed what she didn't want to. *Iske case me toh bhagwanji bhi sure nahi hote ki next kya karegi ye ladki.*

While running away from him, she shouted, "Except for your stupid chewing gum. If you don't stop, I'll just throw you out of this world."

Aakaash smirked. He knew he missed the banter the most and he knew that teasing her was the best part of his day. He just waved at her and signalled her to rush for the meeting first, while he just sat silently and waited for her.

As I always say, if someone waits for you, they do that by choice. Else, not even time waits, forget human beings!

Weirdoes these two were, I am telling you.

ரு

James' room was on the second floor, and without wasting a moment, Tiasha walked up the stairs to his room. Reaching the room in exactly three minutes, she pressed the door bell. He opened the door as he greeted Tiasha with a hug.

Sixty-three years of age and fifty-eight years of editing the world's best magazine on food, James was an epitome of energy and motivation. He never stayed at one place and loved travelling and finding new talent around the globe. With his experience, he was sure to choose the best chefs for his magazine.

He started as Tiasha took a seat in front of him on the couch.

"Tiasha, I was wondering if you would like to join our team?"

Tiasha looked confused. Which team? she wondered.

Pretty puzzled, she asked, "Which team, James?"

He laughed as he replied, "*Cakes and Cuddles,* darling."

Tiasha couldn't believe her ears. Did he just offer her a job in the magazine she dreamt of writing an article for? She was elated with happiness and that smile on her face described it all.

Noticing the smile, James said, "Well, I am not taking you to New York."

The smile became thoughtful. James laughed. Clarifying her confusions, he continued, "Well, we are planning to have an Indian edition of the magazine as we see a market for food related magazines here. We are lagging behind because we don't cater exactly to what the audience wants. Hence, we've decided to open a Head Office in Mumbai. I am offering you to lead the editorial here—that is, if you wish to."

"Of course I wish to, James!" Tiasha exclaimed within a second. Remember, she was impulsive. The job she was working for throughout the night was the decision she took in a second as well. Just that this one probably made sense.

Plus, who wouldn't want their dream job? Adding to it, at twenty-two, if Tiasha led a world-renowned magazine, her career graph would take her places, she knew. She looked cheerful and fortunate. She also knew this opportunity was far precious than the competition. She replied, "I'm on board."

"Awesome. Looking at your working abilities and hearing a lot about how you are juggling with your office and the competition from Rajiv, I was pretty sure you wouldn't be scared of taking up responsibilities. However, let me tell you. This will be very difficult and you will be handling everything independently. You get the budget but ideas flow from your brain. It will be very different from your corporate nine to five job, where you are told what to do. I am sure your tasks would never end here, because you will create them."

Tiasha heard him carefully and then replied, "The only thing that I am sure of at this moment, James, is that I really loved the way I spent my time here the last month. Also, I know I don't want to build someone else's dream. I'd rather build my own house of dreams. And, hard work is something I am never scared of; that's my strength and I know it. Trust me, if I lead the Indian edition, I'll try everything to make it work."

"That's the answer I was expecting, Tiasha. Rajiv told me you'll join the board happily. He will be working with you on the marketing and recipes."

Ah! Tiasha exclaimed. Marketing was fine, but working with Rajiv on recipes was going to be extremely difficult. He was difficult as hell, Tiasha knew. However, the fact that she would get to work with a workaholic excited her. She smiled at the thought and then realised that she couldn't join immediately. She said, "James, just a little problem."

"That the word seems to be deleted from my dictionary long back. Offer me solutions to problems. Anyway, what's it?"

"I still have a month to go in office before I can resign. I would not want to quit a decision to take another," Tiasha said, hesitating a bit and apprehensive of the reaction she would get.

James replied, "I heard of your stubborn nature, little girl. It is very good to be stubborn. I don't have a problem. Like you managed work here, manage the editorial stuff at night for a month and then join. I am good with it."

James was a true businessman. He had become what he was because of his hard work, and therefore, he expected hard work to be the base of any project. He wasn't someone who would emotionally tell Tiasha to get some rest; he would rather grill her further to push her boundaries. He continued, "Go and win the competition. I believe, you've already won. All the best!"

That's all what James said. Sometimes, some people have experience that speaks much more than their words. His trust in Rajiv was pretty logical because he had an experience of a shark and reflexes of an eagle. Rajiv was the perfect choice but Tiasha… that was surprising.

Knowing Rajiv well, he would never suggest someone he considered competition in future and therefore, this decision perhaps was solely James'. This motivated Tiasha further.

Already winning one milestone, Tiasha ran towards the auditorium for her competition, where everyone was waiting for her.

ꝺ

While running, for a millisecond she ran past Aakaash, who stood outside the auditorium, waiting diligently for her for the past hour, while her meeting kept her busy. He knew she was already late for her competition, but he stopped the running Tiasha, holding her wrist and quickly wrapped the apron around her, saying, "Remember, I was to tie the apron around India's best chef one day? I love you, madam."

There was no time for any conversation, there was no time for words to be exchanged. Only togetherness spoke.

As Tiasha just stood there looking in his eyes for a minute, Rajiv rushed out looking for her. When he saw the two of them, he knew that very moment that love was brewing. He smiled, sighing, '*kids*'!

Aakaash realised that their love story could wait a minute, when he said, "*Chal jaa, jeet ke aana.*"

She replied, "I have already won something precious. And you too. Let me now win the competition."

After speaking to Aakaash, as she walked towards Rajiv, he asked while walking briskly towards the kitchen area, "You spoke to James?"

Tiasha smiled, nodding. Rajiv said, "I so didn't want to let a competitor flourish and I tried my best, but your potential proved otherwise. Go, win it here as well."

As he said so, Tiasha laughed. She could now, by experience, know his positivity in the arrogance. She replied to him, "Yes partner."

Winking at him and waving at Aakaash, Tiasha entered the competition.

She did her best, but she did not win. Her dish was delicious but her competitor's dish was better and by that fair chance, Tiasha accepted her defeat with sportsman spirit. Perhaps, at times, in such creative fields, you can't be the best. And not every day is your day. *Theek hai. Aaj koi aur better tha.* You have to make space for the best. Here, Tiasha won a position, but lost the competition, and that's why, she accepted it gracefully.

Rather, she was on cloud nine to be the lead of a magazine's Indian edition. She told her parents and almost played drums about this to everyone. Aakaash stayed by her side, sharing her happiness and being happy with her achievements.

Imperfect misfits

Tiasha and Rajiv were perfect together, but no feeling called love could brew between them. They had similar ideologies, similar aims and a similarly materialistic approach. Yet, they were nothing more than business partners and if I could say, Tiasha was just attracted towards him. However, the moment she had Aakaash, her best friend, by her side, she didn't need anyone else, not even a cigarette. He was her stress-buster and conversations with him were her remedy for every little or large problem.

Aakaash and Aashna were perfect too – she was the personification of care and love. She took care of the most trivial details of his life and made sure they were always together. But, the moment Tiasha's face came to his mind, Aakaash knew it was her he wanted to be with.

True, people say that they were a 'made for each other' couple, they looked 'perfect' together, but in reality, can relationships ever be perfect? I believe each relationship is imperfect and that's what makes it perfect. And just like the dress that might not suit you perfectly at times, some relationships too might not work the way they are supposed to. At times, letting go of the perfect expectations to make things imperfectly perfect becomes important.

Because at times, defining relationships doesn't work. Let them just be *Imperfect Misfits*.

ᔕ

As we talk of big and important aspects like relationships and love and perfect and imperfect, Tiasha resigned from her nine to five job, finally bringing an end to her haphazard schedule. Shifting to Mumbai and then working endlessly with Rajiv throughout the day and night in the magazine office, sleeping less than two hours a day and reporting directly to James about the progress, she was building a brand new magazine for India.

She was working, working and working. Her life started from work and ended at work and that's how she was achieving her dream.

Aakaash was there. She spoke to him about each intricate detail of her life, about little things, about major decisions and steps that she was taking. She was happy to have her best friend back and so was he to have her presence in his life. Thankfully, love was eliminated at least for now. Meanwhile, the equation that Rajiv and Tiasha shared was becoming stronger day by day. His arrogance was becoming subtle and her humility was contagious. Somehow, they were able to work without killing each other and just as she built her dreams and Aakaash built his stand-up career, life kept rotating and revolving around these Imperfect Misfits!

Epilogue

"You know, we kept looking for some memories – good or bad. Never knew we were the memories ourselves."

Aakaash ended his first story on the net. I don't know if you'd believe or not, it went viral within minutes. People loved his story, people loved his ideologies and they respected their relationship. There were tons of comments which spoke about Tiasha and Aakaash and their friendship which brew between love and feelings. They were still best friends, by the way, for they refused to accept the complications and expectations of a relationship. And while the world thought they were perfect together, they were on another unplanned trip. Where they were going, they decided they would decide on their way.

Of course, while Tiasha drove, she fumed,"You love that chewing gum more than me, don't you?"

"Just like you love your cigarette more that you love me," he snapped.

"Of course. It is worth loving. Unlike loving you, you idiot," she replied and the banter continued for years and years.

P.S.: Tiasha was as confused about decisions, but she started taking those risks. Aakaash was the leap taker, which took his channel's reach to triple in the quickest of time! *On and on, life toh perfect nahi hui, ambitions aur dreams ho gaye!*

They roamed the whole world alone, but at the end of each journey, they came back to each other...they came back to their *Imperfect Misfits.*

By the same author

No Matter What I Do...
I end up falling for you

Kabir, Amaira, Kushank and Suhani – four very different people bound together by love and friendship – struggling to find the motto of their lives. Four individuals striving to find themselves. Four threads entangled together and four lives recuperating each other.

No Matter What I Do is the story of these four youngsters, on a journey to find themselves.

The love story narrates tales of reversing stereotypes and finding individuality.

But will they really find their reason to live?